the setup

SMASH POINT SOCIAL
BOOK 2

CYNTHIA GUNDERSON

with gratitude

Editing and Critique
Scott Gunderson

Cover Design
Ink and Veil

Assistants and Sanity Support
Kyra Schroeder, Desri Wulandari

one

I THINK *I might be a sports person.*

That's what I said to Alecia, my ride-or-die best friend, when we pulled up at Smash Point Social at 9 a.m. on New Year's Day. A time I'd normally be sleeping off a hangover or wrapped up in a burrito blanket on my couch, watching the Harry Potter movies from start to finish.

I have no idea how this happened. How I started to love the sound of plastic thwacking on paddles or the smell of court topper—clay? Rubber? All I know is that it gets all over the soles of my shoes and creates gray dust inside the pocket of my bag. The new pickleball bag that Alecia got me for Christmas.

It's only been a couple of months since we started playing at Smash Point Social, all because Alecia wanted to impress Garrett, the founder of Paper and Pixel where we both work, and it already feels like a home away from home. Especially since Alecia ended up falling for her coach instead of her coworker.

We spend a lot of time here, and when I got together with my family over Christmas, it felt like I was trying to hide my recent initiation into a cult. Leaving out the number of times I play each week. Pretending I have friends I see regularly who aren't from the club or that I go out and do things other than open plays or Net Queen round robins on the weekend.

What did we do before we had pickleball?

The game on Court Five ends, and I'm invited to jump in with a friend, Drew, who's been waiting with me for an opening. We won't get to play together since the winners have to stay on the court and split. That's unfortunate. I love playing with Drew. He's happy and chill. Doesn't get mad if I mess up a point. He reminds me of my best friend in college, Adam. He has a similar smile, and there's something about the way he moves, a little lopey in his gait.

You'd think that would make me never want to see him again, considering I can't see Adam anymore. But somehow it's more comforting than sad.

Alecia waves to me from Court Four. She and Calder aren't playing in the open play. They have another couple they've been scheduling game time with to help them prepare for a tournament. Alecia still isn't good enough to partner competitively with Calder, but that's absolutely her end goal. And when she puts her mind to something, it's only a matter of time.

"Hey. Ready?" Samir, a guy I've played with many times in open play holds out a paddle, and I tap it.

"Yep. Let's go." I serve first, and the game begins. It's a rush of both excitement and terror each time I approach the net, though the ratio is skewing less terror each week. I'm improving steadily, and seeing that progress is more exciting than most things in my life.

I'm good at my job. I'm good at running my life.

I didn't know how boring that was until I found something I wasn't good at and started working at it.

"Nice." Samir nods in approval as I block a volley and send the ball to Drew's feet. He gets it back, but the ball flies high enough, Samir is able to slam it to the back corner.

Maybe I also enjoy the influx of compliments? I don't consider myself a people pleaser, but it does feel nice to be recognized every once in awhile. Especially since, for the past three months, I've been inundated with Calder and Alecia's ooey-gooey relationship.

I love that they love each other. I'm also living on a diet of half our usual text messages and social events. We still have our Wednesday dinners, and thank goodness we see each other regularly here at Smash Point. But I'm a little attention-starved.

We play out the game, tying once at 11-11, then barely losing 14-12. A solid showing. I thank the other three for the game and hop off the court.

"You have any plans this weekend?" Drew asks as we exit through the gate in the fence. It's a benign question considering he has a girlfriend of over two years. It's also mostly rhetorical since we both know I'll be here at the club. More than usual, actually, since my holiday rebrand for a regional nonprofit, including six weeks of Pantone approvals, recycled 120-lb uncoated stock, and a last-minute save on a misaligned foil stamp over the holidays, closes on the third.

I shrug. "Just the regular. Net Queens, maybe Midnight Madness on Friday. You?"

Drew frowns. "You're kidding, right?" He wipes his brow with a towel from his bag. "It was a joke. I assumed you were coming with everyone to the tournament in the Springs."

It takes me a minute, but I finally connect the dots. Alecia had given me the run-down before Christmas. A two-day pickleball tournament in Colorado Springs, the first of four in each Four Corners state, run by Justin's company, Baseline Collective. It's Saturday and Sunday, indoor courts, men's and women's singles on Saturday, mixed and gender doubles on Sunday, round-robin pools with playoffs, capped at twelve teams per division.

My mind is a lock box. Except when it ignores dates. *That's this weekend?*

My heart picks up speed. *Dammit.* Alecia and Calder are going—hell, half our friends from the club are going because Justin, the owner's son from Smash Point, is one of the organizers.

I try to hide my surprise. "Wow, that's this weekend already? How is it already the new year?" I avoid commenting on my attendance because I don't have a good explanation for why I won't be there. Well, I have a good explanation for myself. Just not one that most people would deem socially appropriate.

My favorite romance series ever is being made into a TV series, and the first five episodes drop on Netflix Friday at midnight. On Saturday, I have a date with my couch.

Drew takes a swig from his stainless steel water bottle. "I know. January seemed so far away when I signed up."

"You're competing?"

He nods, pointing to a petite woman in an adorable plum colored tennis outfit. "Shana and I are playing mixed 3.0-3.5."

Doubles. Something twinges beneath my ribs. I've had a few guys and girls ask if I wanted to play with them. I even had a few offers to sign up as partners for the tournament this weekend. But the idea of doing anything official, of potentially letting someone down with a DUPR rating on the line, makes me want to crawl into a hole.

I was gung-ho about getting a DUPR ranking when I first started, but then I heard people talking on the courts. How they played competitive events when they first started and now their ranking was low. How they tried to bring it up, but the algorithm slotted them in one range, and they couldn't make it move to reflect their new skill level. How they played with a partner who choked and it tanked their ranking.

No, thank you.

I smile at Drew. "Sounds like a blast. I'm sure you'll do great." The other games are still going, so I take a break and jog to the bathroom and refill my water bottle.

When I exit the locker room area and start down the aisle between the courts, I slow at a small congregation outside the gate to Alecia's court. Alecia stands with a hand on her hip, talking with Natasha, Ben, the woman from the couple they were just playing, and Calder.

"I can't believe that." Natasha shakes her head. "There are a thousand other options. You know she did it on purpose."

My curiosity is piqued, and I lean in.

"Right? Which means she's still into him. People don't do crap like that unless they want attention and validation from their ex." Alecia notices I'm there and fills me in on the details. "Justin's ex. Minnie."

My eyes widen. "Quite the name." I'm not particularly invested in Justin's love life. He's always putting on a show when he's here at Smash Point, and I'm sure plenty of women get sucked into that high-energy BS. For me, it's a little too multi-level marketing.

"It's a nickname," Natasha says.

"She's running a tournament at the same time and place as Justin's Four Corners," Alecia says.

I frown. That seems like a dick move. "She runs tournaments, too?" The whole infrastructure of this sport confuses me. There are official organizations, official rankings, and private groups that run tournaments across the country with their own rules for everything from age, DUPR, and paddle type. It seems they'd benefit from a bit more standardization, like a Nicene Council of pickleball.

Calder huffs a breath. "That's how they met. They worked for the same group."

Alecia nods. "Prestige Pickleball. Then Justin did his own thing."

Ben leans on the fence. "He built his company from scratch because he was annoyed with how exorbitant the fees were with Prestige."

"Plus the disorganization," Natasha adds.

I fail to see the issue. "If they're at the same time, won't everyone sign up for Justin's then?" If it was cheaper, I definitely would.

Calder shakes his head. "You don't sign up. You qualify. And because of their fees, the pot for winners is higher with Prestige."

"Plus, they do crazy marketing and always bring in big-time names like Amy Lee Lake," Alecia says. I smirk, loving how much this has become her personality since she started dating Calder.

She catches the look and fights off a smile, sending a look of her own that says, *I know, I know. I'm ridiculous.*

"I think Finn Johnson is going to be there this year," Ben says.

Finn Johnson. The thirty-year-old pickleball pro who people talk about like he's a demigod. To be fair, I've never watched him play, but it's on my list.

"He definitely is," Calder mutters, and the rest of the group quiets. When he realizes we're all staring, he says, "Because he and Minnie are together."

Alecia's jaw drops. "Shut up."

Natasha makes a sound in her throat. "Well, that explains it. She's doing all of that just to flaunt a new boyfriend?"

I have no horse in this race. I've never had more than a two-word conversation with Justin, but since Calder is friends with him, Alecia has a stronger vested interest.

Alecia's face falls. "Oh, that sucks."

Calder nods. "Yep."

"Have you talked to him?" she asks.

Calder runs a hand over the back of his neck. "He's been slammed getting ready for Four Corners. Haven't had a chance."

"That means it's going to kick him in the nuts when he's down there." Ben taps his paddle against his hip.

"Well." Alecia draws a deep breath. "We'll just need to be moral support, right? Try to make it as painless as possible." She turns to me. "Sam, I really think you should come. I'm not playing either—"

"No, I'm good. I've got plans." I give her the look that says, *We talked about this, and you know I don't fancy being the third wheel to your and Calder's tandem.*

Her eyes narrow, and I know she's saying, *I'm not your only friend here, and there are plenty of single people going to this tournament.*

She's trying to be nice, and I do appreciate it. But regardless of the effort she's putting in to make sure I don't feel excluded, her life is expanding to include another best friend. One with whom she can have sex, so he automatically wins.

I don't want to be the needy best friend. Which is why I'm giving them their space. "Good luck with the whole Justin and Minnie thing," I say, starting off toward the open play courts.

My watch buzzes against my wrist, and I flip the face up to look at it. My brows pinch as I read.

NOTICE OF PLANNED OUTAGE: Power will be temporarily shut off at your address on Saturday, 8:00 a.m. to 6:00 p.m. and Sunday 8:00 a.m. to 2:00 p.m. to allow crews to replace aging transformers and upgrade safety equipment. We appreciate your patience as we complete this necessary work to improve reliability in your area.

I hiss air through my teeth. "What?!"

two

"WHAT IS IT?" Alecia runs up to stand next to me.

I look up, shoving my watch in front of her. "A power outage. At my complex."

She reads the text. "How can they do that? It's basically the whole weekend." She looks up, gives me the appropriate pitying look, but she's fighting a smile.

I raise an eyebrow. "Did you do this?"

"What? How could I plan a power outage to an entire complex?" Alecia laughs out loud.

"I don't know. It seems like something you would do."

She crosses her arms. "Or maybe this is the universe telling you that you're supposed to come to the Springs."

"The universe doesn't care whether I drive down to a pickleball tournament."

Alecia shrugs. "Has this ever happened before?"

"No."

"And it just happens to land on the tournament weekend . . ." She takes a step back toward the fence.

"Any weekend it landed on would be something to do with pickleball, A. We're here all the time."

"I'm just saying." She holds out her hands, looking to the others for moral support, then stills when someone approaches from the front desk.

"Hey, hey." Justin stops next to Ben. "You're all coming to the Springs with me, I hear."

My friends' faces light up.

"Wouldn't miss it," Natasha says.

Ben claps him on the shoulder. "You're making sure the net cord rolls go our direction, right?"

Justin grins. "Always." He looks up at me. "Are you coming, Sam? I don't think I saw your name on the list."

I'm not sure how to answer that. Five minutes ago, I would've easily given my apologies, but now that my power will be out all weekend? I'm still not even close to a hundred percent, but I'm no longer at zero. All my friends from the club will be gone, and I'll have only my battery-powered laptop and phone to keep me entertained.

Also, I'm slightly distracted by the fact that he knows my name. Have I ever had a real conversation with him that didn't start with "Looks like you're working on that back-hand!" I swear he has five lines he runs on loop while walking the aisles of Smash Point.

"She's thinking about it," Alecia says with a grin. "Due to *none* of my own meddling."

Justin's mouth quirks. "Sounds like there's a backstory there."

"There isn't." I take another step away from the group.

"Sam!" Drew calls my name from two courts over. Saved.

I wave my paddle with a "See you all later," then make a beeline for my court.

The last hour of open play takes my mind off the atrocity that is my powerless apartment this weekend. But by the time we're packing up, I'm already wondering whether I'll be able to shower with hot water.

"Do water heaters work without electricity?" I ask Alecia as she pulls out of the parking lot.

Alecia makes a face. "No idea. I don't think I knew I had a hot water heater. Wait, do we have one? Or is there just one for the building?"

I laugh. "Yes, for the building. But do they work?"

"Ask a chat bot."

I pull out my phone and query. "It says it depends on whether it's old or new. If it's only gas or if it uses electricity." I try to remember when my building was finished. Not long enough to be considered old.

I drop my phone in my lap and groan. "So I can't shower either?"

"Maybe if you got up early?"

I turn my head to look at her. "Don't pretend you're not gleeful about this."

"I'm not! I'm trying to troubleshoot."

"You're grinning at the idea of me sitting there in the dark like a Victorian orphan."

"It wasn't just orphans who didn't have electricity during Victorian times."

"Well, I don't even have candles!"

She scoffs. "We can remedy that. One stop at Anthropologie—"

I chortle. "Yes. I need forty-dollar Volcano emergency candles, please."

"I feel like 'orphan' is a mindset you're actively adopting now." She crosses the highway and turns right toward my street. "Also, candles are very brand-aligned for you. Moody. Dramatic."

I slump into the seat. "I guess that's true."

"Ooh! You could boil water on the stove and pour yourself a proper bath!"

"Stop!" She's getting way too into this. But I am laughing, so there's that.

"It's too bad you hate being alone," she says.

"I don't hate being alone."

"Okay, well, you tolerate it. Like unsalted almonds."

I snort. "That's uncalled for." I may have pretended to like the almonds she brought me at work when I complained I didn't have healthy office snacks. Even though they tasted like tree bark.

"You're a terrible liar." She pulls up to the curb outside my apartment.

I grab for the door handle. "Thanks for driv—"

"We aren't finished with this conversation, young lady."

I freeze, and Alecia's eyes light up.

"Holy shit. That worked." Her smile is approaching Christmas morning levels. "Text me when you make a decision. And there *is* a right and a wrong choice here."

"Got it. Anything else?"

She nods soberly. "Make sure he wears protection, and make sure you wear clean underwear!" Alecia yells the last part because I've already exited the vehicle.

I turn back and flip her the bird. She pretends it's a blown kiss and slaps it to her cheek.

I laugh as I walk into my building.

I love her.

Which is why I'll say yes to the stupid tournament.

* * *

I slide into my office chair on Wednesday and open my email. After answering a few messages, I spend the next three hours finishing the holiday rebrand. Six weeks of approvals, revisions, and supply chain miracles.

When I hit send on the last confirmation, I sit back, close my eyes, and draw a deep breath.

Done. Biggest account of the season, and it went off without more than five hitches.

I'm about to break for lunch when a message pops up on my screen. It's from Garrett and has the subject line of "Senior Designer/Creative Strategist Considerations." My heart kicks up into high speed. There haven't been any major promotions here in over a year and a half, and I didn't think this position would be open, possibly ever. *Was Margo retiring?* Had another company headhunted her?

I lean in and read the body text, hoping for clarifying details, but I'm disappointed. There's only information about the job and ideal candidates.

. . . must demonstrate leadership on an independently driven account with measurable ROI. Preference given to projects with community impact . . .

I scroll through the job requirements, then suck in a breath when I see the pay scale. It's a significant upgrade. But my current accounts? All team-based. January is a dead zone. No one onboards new clients during budget limbo, and—

Alecia bursts through the door. "Did you see it?"

"Yes, I saw it," I murmur, still staring at the screen.

"Aaaaand you're definitely going to apply, right?" She strides in and perches on the edge of my desk.

"A. I don't qualify."

Alecia leans in. "So qualify."

"It's not that easy. I have zero independent projects."

"Incorrect. You have zero independent projects *yet*."

I clear the remnants of mandarin orange peel from my desk and throw them in the trash. When I look back at Alecia, she's grinning like she's waiting for me to figure out she got her hair cut. "What?"

She hops down from the desk. "Who do you know who runs a fast-growing business with strong community impact, recurring events, and zero marketing infrastructure?"

I bark a laugh. "Nobody."

She shrugs, but her eyes drop to the industrial carpet. The tell-tale sign that she's not telling me everything.

"Alecia—"

"Let's start looking, then. Shouldn't be too hard to find, right?"

She doesn't give me anything for the rest of the day or on our way to Wednesday dinner. We opt for Thai take-out and sit cross-legged on her couch, our cartons open and steaming on the coffee table.

She pokes at her noodles. "Okay. Say you don't go to the Springs. What do you do?"

"Read."

Alecia snorts. We both know that's not happening. I'm an audiobook-only girl.

"And if you do go?" she asks.

"I follow you and Calder around like a sad puppy."

"Stop. You're not pathetic."

I raise an eyebrow and take a bite of my rice and basil pork.

"You know lots of single people from Smash Point," she

continues. "I'm sure they'll be doing dinner and sitting at the bar after the games. It'll be a blast."

I love that she's trying to encourage me, but it's not the people I know or don't know at Smash Point that are the problem. Since Alecia got together with Calder, I've become painfully aware of how codependent I am.

I'm not like Alecia. I've never been one to make a gaggle of friends, to collect people everywhere I go. I'm patient. I wait to find my person, and when I do, I cling on tight.

My throat constricts.

It's been years, but I remember exactly what it felt like to lose Adam. Two weeks ago was the first time I'd dreamed about his funeral since 2023.

"Ooh!" Alecia nearly drops her fork. "What if you text Leah?"

That comment gives me whiplash, and it takes me a second to remember Leah is my cousin. "Why?"

"To see if you could stay with her in the Springs! Then you could come to the tournament, but if it wasn't fun, you could hang out with family."

I consider that. Not the worst idea. Alecia grins as I pull out my phone and tap out a quick message.

We finish eating while watching the second half of *The Holiday* because neither of us had time to watch it over Christmas.

I'm about to clean up our trash when my phone buzzes.

Leah:

> I wish 😭 I'm out of town until Monday.
> Sorry, Sam!

"Is that Leah?" Alecia leans over to see the message.

"Yep. Out of town." I scroll to my maps app. "Where is everyone staying?" I figure I should probably put her out of her misery and tell her I already accepted my fate, but she's still coming up with excellent backup plans.

Alecia scoots closer. "We're staying at the Summit Lodge, but I think there's overflow at the Pikes Peak Conference Center." She puts out a finger and scrolls further east from the Colorado Springs city center. "The tournament is at the Fieldhouse. Kind of out in the boonies."

From what I've heard, Front Range Fieldhouse is all function. Retrofitted from an old warehouse, the place has eighteen indoor courts with high ceilings and no frills.

"Here, you check and see how much the Conference Center costs, and I'll see if there's any availability at Summit Lodge." Alecia locks in on her task, and I don't call her on being a little too eager. It feels good that she wants me to be there, even if I'm worried I'll be an inconvenience.

I tap into the Pikes Peak Conference Center website and enter my dates. The wheel spins, then loads a screen with the words "No matches found." I frown. This is a conference center. How could it be—

"Full." Alecia frowns. "What did you find?"

I turn my screen to face her.

She makes a sympathetic noise, then straightens. "It's because of Prestige. Because there are two tournaments in the same place this weekend."

Her lips purse, and I know that expression. I've seen it in meetings and in the middle of Target aisles. It's the physical manifestation of Alecia's internal decision to problem-solve at all costs.

I try to cut her future efforts off at the knees. "It's fine. I don't need—"

"No. I refuse to let you sit alone in a dark apartment eating peanut butter like a raccoon."

"I wouldn't eat it with a spoon! I have crackers!"

She shoots me a look, and her thumbs are already flying. "Raccoons don't even use spoons."

"What are you doing?"

She doesn't look up. "Hypothetically, if there were a hotel suite with an extra—"

"No."

"A bed. Not floor space."

"No."

"But it's people you already know."

"I don't play well with others."

Alecia laughs. "Nice try." She taps the side of her phone, waiting for something. Then her face lights up. "Okay, so yes. There's a suite at the hotel. Two bedrooms, plus a living area."

"Alecia."

She steamrolls ahead, staring me down. "Rachel and Brooke booked it. You know them. Super normal. Super fun. Rachel works in product management for a fitness app, and she runs a lot of the junior programming at the club. Brooke does nonprofit development, I think? You've talked to both of them."

I have. And it's true that they do seem normal. But looks can be deceiving.

"There are already a couple of people staying there, but there's a sofa bed in the living room. They'd only charge you twenty-five dollars a night."

My eyebrows raise. "That's absurdly cheap."

"They get that it's not ideal."

I open my mouth to argue and then close it again.

"You don't have to stay all weekend if it sucks. But at

least come out for the first night. Justin's doing this kick-off party. It's going to be a blast." She waits a beat, then says, "And you could charge up all your devices."

three

I SAY YES. How could I not after she went through all that trouble? Which was, I'm sure, her intention all along. But that's why we make a good team. I make sure she doesn't fall for internet scams, and she drags me into adventures I'd never say yes to otherwise.

I'm sitting in the back of Calder's car, not Alecia's, because the snow came in sideways overnight, and his has all-wheel drive.

They're talking about some errand Calder said he'd run for Justin once they arrive, trying to determine whether it would be best to do before dinner or after.

Every few lines, Alecia glances up in the rearview mirror to check in on me, and I hate that she's worried I might feel left out. Worse, I hate that she feels responsible for me when she should just be enjoying this time with Calder.

I want her to prioritize time with me, and I simultaneously want her not to prioritize time with me. I want her to feel both guilty and totally free to be with Calder. I want everything to go back to normal, and I want her to be so happy in this relationship.

So. My feelings are pretty straightforward these days.

"Wait, Sam, did you hear what happened with Megan and the client yesterday?"

I jump in with both feet. "No, was it bad?"

"She accidentally sent it in the wrong font."

I groan. "No."

"She had to recall the entire deck and—"

We slide a little at a stoplight, and Alecia tries to press into the dash as Calder throws out a hand across her chest, pressing her back against the seat.

"You good?" He asks as the car finally grips asphalt.

She nods, wrapping her hand around his.

Then she turns to the backseat.

* * *

Calder pulls into the Summit Lodge lot just as the snow starts up again. Big flakes, wet and heavy, sticking to the windshield. He parks crooked since the lines are already close to invisible, corrects, then shuts the engine off.

We climb out, and the wind pushes the flakes sideways, straight down the collar of my coat. Calder tries to take all our bags in, but Alecia insists on rolling hers. I only have my overnight duffel, and he refuses to pass that over. I give in, duck my head, and jog, boots slipping once on the painted curb before I catch myself.

"Don't die!" Alecia laughs as we trundle into the rotating glass doors.

Inside, the Lodge smells like coffee and firewood. The floor is tiled and slick from tracked-in snow, but it's cozy with a gas fireplace crackling along one wall and plush upholstered furniture staged in the lobby.

The whole place is buzzing. It's just past four o'clock,

and there must be some kind of happy hour deal going on because the restaurant and adjoining bar are both packed.

Alecia and Calder veer toward the check-in desk, dragging their rolling bags and my duffel. I don't know if the hotel staff are aware that I'm joining the suite, so I plan to wait until Brooke or Rachel comes down.

I park myself in an armchair and resist the urge to pull out my phone. One of my New Year's resolutions. To try to be less uncomfortable when I'm alone in public places.

Without staring, I scan the crowd in the restaurant. Most people have to be from the tournament because I've never seen a more athletic display.

"Hey, Calder!" someone calls from the bar.

He turns from the check-in desk and smiles when he sees who was trying to get his attention. He says something to Alecia, then leaves the bags and walks off to join the fray.

From what I can tell, Calder and Justin have been friends for a while. Even before Calder started working at Smash Point. Not that I was paying much attention, but with so many people talking about Justin and his split from Prestige Pickleball, I have a general understanding of what happened.

Justin ran tournaments with Prestige until his goals no longer aligned with the corporate vision, then he split off and started his own thing: Baseline Collective. He's been trying to get it off the ground, but from what Alecia said, it's been an uphill battle. With how popular the sport has become, it seems everyone and their dog has decided to try their hand at running leagues and tournaments.

"Checked in," Alecia announces, dragging both bags over. Including mine looped over Calder's handle. I stand and retrieve it.

"Brooke and Rachel are coming down," she says.

"Perfect."

Alecia steps closer. "Did you see all the hot guys at the bar?"

I roll my eyes, and she laughs. We both know that means I definitely did.

Calder breaks free of the group he was pulled into and starts toward us just as Brooke and Rachel exit the elevator and scan the lobby.

I wave, my heart picking up speed. This is fine. I'll just . . . share a bathroom. And sleep in the open, where people might walk through my room in the middle of the night to get a glass of water. I updated my white noise app and brought a sleep mask. *It will be fine.*

Alecia squeezes my arm. "Text me when you're settled? We can meet up for dinner before the party?"

"Go to dinner with Calder. I'll be fine."

Before she can argue, Brooke and Rachel stop next to us.

"Roomie!" Rachel throws her arms out, and I hug her, then move on to Brooke.

"So glad you could come!" Brooke says.

"Me, too. Thanks for sheltering me."

Rachel chortles. "The least we could do." She hands me a keycard. "We have some snacks up there, but if you need anything, there is a little store on the other side of the parking lot. Supes expensive."

Alecia's lips quirk, and I give her a look that says, *You're making me room with someone who shortens barely two-syllable words?*

I'm sure Rachel's a cool person. I decide to forgive her, hoping there won't be a repeat offense.

I lift my duffel and give Alecia a hug. "Enjoy dinner. We'll talk tomorrow."

"First thing," she says. "Breakfast in the restaurant at seven?"

I groan, but give her a nod, then follow Brooke and Rachel to the elevators. Rachel's tall and athletic with her dark hair pulled into a high ponytail and a double piercing in her ears. Brooke is shorter with platinum-blonde hair in a low bun, an oversized sweater layered over leggings.

I've seen them play at Smash Point a few times. Both of them are intermediate to advanced players, but Rachel's more intimidating. I've never seen someone successfully lob her.

"So." Brooke looks back over her shoulder. "First tournament?"

I nod.

"Are you playing?" Rachel asks, pressing the button to call for the lift.

"Hell, no."

Brooke snorts. "Honestly, I wish I'd observed at my first tournament. I completely tanked. So nervous."

The door to the elevator beside us opens, and we step in. Both of them are easy to talk to, and by the time we reach our room, I know a little more about Rachel's wellness app—I honestly need it for myself—and Brooke's latest grant application. I have a thousand questions for both of them, but as Rachel scans her card and opens the door, all of them fizzle on my tongue.

I blink, trying to make sense of the scene in front of me.

Justin is standing at the counter of a kitchenette. He's shirtless, his athletic shorts riding low enough on his hips, his hip bone divots are on full display.

"Oh, hey. That was quick." He pulls the wrapper off his protein bar and takes a bite. "Welcome home, Sam."

four

MY BRAIN ABSORBS every detail in sections. Justin in our room. Justin's chest hair. Small table, spacious living area. Justin's backward hat. Justin turning. His arm flex as he flicks on the tap to fill a glass of water. There's a TV and a coffee table. Justin, staring at me because he just asked me something, and I have no idea what it was.

"Sorry, what?" I ask. Alecia said there were a few people staying here, but did she know it was Justin?

"Geez, let her get in the room first." Brooke moves aside so I can squeeze through the doorframe with my overnight bag.

I walk past the abs display to my right and pretend to inspect the art print on the wall above the couch. It looks too phallic to be an accident.

"That's a big ass purse." Justin takes a bite of the protein bar that's roughly the size of a cinder block. Chews. Swallows.

Rachel laughs. "Hilarious." She kicks off her shoes and walks into the room. "The pull-out's actually decent. It's not the spring kind. It's memory foam or something."

Justin's eyebrows lift. "We have a sofa bed?"

I glance between the three of them. "Did you not know I was coming?"

Justin shakes his head, but Rachel waves him off. "I texted you."

He takes another bite. "Must've missed it."

I have so many questions. Why is Justin, as the tournament organizer, staying in a room with other people? And why Rachel and Brooke?

I would've assumed Justin booked it and the girls are tagging along, but he doesn't seem the least bit in charge here.

The suite is great. Two bedrooms connected by a short hall. Living room with my couch-slash-sofa bed. Water bottles, keys, and one lonely pickleball paddle colonize the short kitchenette counter, and someone's jacket slumps over a chair at the table.

Justin clears his throat as he leans down to throw his protein bar wrapper in the trash. "Sorry. If I'd known you were coming, I would've been fully clothed."

"Ah. Topless is only for Rachel and Brooke?" I say without thinking, and his eyes widen.

Rachel snorts. "He's basically a brother to me. It has zero effect."

Justin looks taken aback. "Zero effect? That's a bit extreme."

She laughs. "Aw! Your ego is that fragile? You need me to be secretly attracted to you?"

Okay. So, I love her.

Justin blows out a breath, his usual smile landing on his face. "I didn't know someone else was staying with us. That's all I was saying."

"Well, I won't hold it against you. I didn't know I was getting you as a roommate either."

His brow ticks. "Cool. We can endure this surprise together, then."

It's like someone shoved a spatula under my ribs and flipped my stomach like a pancake. He's a flirt. Obviously. I just need to ignore him, and he'll go away.

"Right." I look down at my bag, then at the couch. "Should we—"

"Oh, yeah. I'll get the sheets from the closet," Brooke offers.

We pull out the bed and set it up, then Rachel and Brooke head to their room to get ready for dinner. They invite me, and my knee-jerk reaction is to decline since I already declined with Alecia. But if I wanted to sit alone at home, I could've done that in my powerless apartment. But this hotel room has a bonus shirtless man . . .

I draw a deep breath and shake that image from my head. "Sure." Then I plug in all three of my devices.

"Rachel was with one of my best friends for two years."

I jump at the sound of Justin's voice. He's back in the kitchen, with a shirt on this time. I stand with my knees against the bed, hugging my toiletry bag to my middle. "Oh?"

"Yeah." He runs a hand over the back of his neck. "Bad breakup. Still kind of awkward when he's in town, but she's great. I wasn't going to pick a side."

I nod.

"But I don't—it was never like *that* between us. We're just good friends. And Brooke plays at Smash Point. She and Rachel are like this." He loops his pointer and middle fingers.

"Good to know." Why was he telling me this? Did I give the impression that I cared about his relationships?

"Just wanted you to know nothing weird was going to go down."

"Oh. Right. Weird like . . . sex?"

He coughs a laugh. "Yeah."

"It turns out I'm an adult, so—"

"No, I know. I just—that's not what this is. So you don't have to worry."

"I wasn't worried."

"Right." He presses his palms into the counter, and I find myself imagining the pose with ten minutes ago, Justin. Sans T-shirt.

I shake my head and round the bed, then stop when I reach the threshold between the living area and the kitchen. There's no bathroom in the common area. Which means—

"You can use my bathroom." He points to the bedroom on my right. "Less traffic."

I don't question it, but when I walk in and shut the door behind me, I wonder if I should've asked more questions. Should I leave my toiletries here? Take them with me? I hate carting my whole bag around, but I doubt he'd enjoy having me take over half the counter.

"Just leave your stuff in there! I don't mind!" he calls from the bedroom.

Surprising that a guy would think to clarify that point, but I'll take it.

I scan the counter and shower. It's tidy. Toothbrush in a case. Razor clean and plugged in. A travel bottle of face wash, and towels hung up, not piled on the floor.

The last time I shared a bathroom with a guy, it was Adam, and we were both nineteen. He was an absolute mess, but so clueless about it that I couldn't get mad. I just hung up his towels and picked up the flossers on the floor when he missed the trash. I did snap at him once or twice when he used my deodorant because he forgot to buy any.

I regret that now.

I empty out my toiletries, and it isn't until I dry my hands on the hand towel that I see it.

A tube of hand cream in the corner. Green label. Same brand.

I freeze, my breath lodging in my throat.

Adam used that hand cream. I remember the smell. Rich and creamy, peppermint and hemp. He'd slather it on his hands, then snatch mine without asking and say, "It's a gift. Take it like a good girl." It sounds aggressive, but Adam was anything but. He was goofy and kind and the least threatening person on the planet.

I laugh to myself at the memory, then swallow hard as my eyes prick.

Adam was suffering silently, and I—his best friend and sometimes roommate—had zero clue.

I hate that I had zero clue.

When I step out of the bathroom, Justin's resting on the bed, looking at something on his phone.

He lifts his head, but doesn't move to get up. "How are the accommodations?"

"Perfect. Thanks." I fight the urge to squirm under his gaze. I'm alone with him in his bedroom, and he's stretched out, his arm behind his head.

He drops his phone to the comforter. "Why'd you decide to come?"

I wet my lips. "Because I have a thing for sofa beds."

He laughs out loud. "Don't we all." He cocks his head to the side. "You're playing?"

"Uh, no."

"Here to hang with Alecia and Calder, then?"

"Pretty much. My apartment had a planned power outage this weekend."

"Well, I was going to say. Alecia and Calder are barely better than a power outage, so . . . "

I huff a laugh. "The obvious comparison."

"That's how I judge all my friends. On a scale of power outage to EDM and pacifiers—"

"Who makes EDM and pacifiers level?"

"Rachel. Definitely."

I laugh just as Rachel yells, "Are you talking about me?"

"Always," Justin calls back.

She appears at the door with Brooke in tow. Their coats are on, cheeks rosy. I wish I'd spent less time looking at Justin's hand cream and more time making myself look cute.

"Is he harassing you?" Brooke asks.

I nod soberly. "I was about to get out my pepper spray."

Rachel's face lights up. "Ooh, can I watch?"

Justin scoffs. "You've obviously never used pepper spray before. No, you can't watch, or it'll get in your eyes, too."

Brooke gapes. "Have you been sprayed before?"

"No, but--"

"Then how do you know?" she asks.

"It's common sense."

"He's mansplaining pepper spray," Rachel says, planting a hand on her hip.

Justin rolls his eyes. "You can't say mansplaining anytime I talk."

"Don't mansplain every time you talk, and I won't." She flashes a cheesy smile, then walks over to the bed and plants a kiss on his forehead. "Don't stay out too late. You have an early morning tomorrow."

He sighs. "But our new roommate says she's an adult and she's fine if I have sex—"

I splutter something that sounds like "No, I didn't!" but technically, I did say something like that. "Not in that context," I explain. "He brought it up."

Rachel slaps his shoulder, and Justin laughs. "I'm kidding!" He turns and winks at me, and a flush creeps up my neck. I have no doubt that he'd have plenty of offers if he walked down to the bar and existed for more than five minutes.

Since I can't think of a witty comeback, I stride to the door. "I'll grab my coat." My face is still burning as I walk to the edge of the bed and grab my things. So much for ignoring him. He's funny and charismatic, which are two things I'm normally immune to. But then again, I don't often find myself trapped in an apartment with them.

I text Alecia and let her know I'll probably see her later, then meet Brooke and Rachel at the door. We head off, making our way through the hotel and out the back. There's a restaurant next to the aforementioned grocery store, and the smell of burgers and queso hits us square in the face as we push through the storm doors.

Rachel grabs the menu and starts narrating options. We debate between the taco salad, fire alarm burger, and the fajitas, then decide to get one of each so we can try them all.

When the server leaves, I keep my voice casual. "So. Why is Justin not in his own room?"

Rachel takes a chip from the basket the server dropped in front of us, drenching it in salsa. "He never rooms on his own at these things if he can help it. He hates wasting money."

I must look surprised because Brooke jumps in. "It's one of the things he hated most about Prestige. That they spent stupid amounts of money on the staff, then raised their registration fees."

This surprises me. The Justin I keep hearing about from Alecia, and now Rachel and Brooke, doesn't align with the Justin I see at Smash Point. He's always the center of attention. Always dressed nicely, product in his hair, the nicest pickleball bags, and pristine athletic wear.

"Hm. He doesn't come off as frugal."

Rachel snorts. "Yeah. He hates that sponsorship shit." She dips another chip. "He has companies sending him stuff all the time, hoping he'll promote it at his tournaments. Not the really pricy brands, but the mid-level ones. I think he has twelve paddles at this point."

Huh. Again, not what I expected.

"I don't think the pricy ones will ever send him stuff," Brooke says. "They're all in bed with Minnie."

"Okay, what's the deal with all that?" I ask. Alecia's told me the story, but I want to hear it from their perspective. From people who have known him longer than we have.

Rachel sighs. "Minnie isn't evil. She had a rough life growing up, and she learned to get what she wanted."

"Well . . . " Brooke purses her lips. "At some point, we all need to grow up."

"No, agreed." Rachel leans her arms on the table. "There's no way she'll be able to hold a healthy relationship until she figures out how to be happy with herself." Rachel loops me in with some context. "She was always cutting Justin down. Criticizing him, blaming him for things that were completely outside of his control. I hated watching it."

Brooke nods. "I only saw the last bit of it, but it was bad." She crunches a chip. "Remember when she showed up at Smash Point right after he split from Prestige? Cussed him out in the entryway?"

My eyes widen. "What?"

Rachel gives me a look. "Yeah. She did not like that he was moving on."

Again, this all hits a little too close to home. Adam's last two relationships were like that before he passed. He was always apologizing, making excuses. I tried to tell him that he deserved someone who treated him well. Someone who thought the sun shone out his ass just like he believed about those girls, but he couldn't see it. My brother used to be a little like that, too. Thankfully, he figured it out before he met his now wife on a flight to Taipei.

I want to ask more questions about the whole Justin and Minnie situation, but the server arrives at the table with our food, and then we're talking about how to split everything up with the extra plates he brought.

The conversation winds from dating to pickleball to work and back again. We somehow finish all three dishes we ordered and debate getting dessert before looking at the clock and realizing it's almost nine.

Welcome party started an hour ago in the bar, but we all have to be up early. We opt for the truffles Brooke brought and stashed back at the hotel room, split our bill three ways, and trek back across the snow-covered parking lot.

The wind picked up while we were eating, and it bites against my cheeks as we rush to the back door of the hotel. It makes the warm air feel heavenly as we enter the hall. It's so quiet inside, we lower our voices, especially when we hear what sounds like a tense conversation drifting toward us from farther down the hall.

Just as I'm about to round the corner, Rachel grabs my arm. I start, and she puts a finger to her lips.

"I just don't understand why you're doing this to yourself," a woman's voice says. "This isn't ever going to be as big as Prestige."

Rachel mouths, "Minnie," and my eyes widen.

"It's going well. I'm happy with where I'm at." Justin's voice. *Holy crap.* I feel a little guilty eavesdropping, but at the same time, I strain to hear every syllable.

Minnie laughs. Mocking. "I'm sure you are."

"I'm not trying to—"

"You never try to," she cuts in. "That's the problem."

"I'm sorry," Justin says. "I didn't mean for this to be uncomfortable."

Rachel's eyes flash. Another mouthed sentence. *"He's apologizing?"*

As far as I understood, he had nothing to apologize for. Alecia said he booked everything for his Four Corners tournament before Minnie or Prestige ever announced theirs.

Rachel pulls me forward, and I grab onto Brooke. We round the corner together, Rachel laughing at some pretend joke, and we follow suit.

Justin's back is to us, and he doesn't turn, but Minnie looks our direction. She's . . . stunning. Petite with jet black hair, a perfectly symmetrical face with deep brown eyes. She's wearing a cocktail dress and heels that show off her very well-moisturized legs.

She turns her attention back to Justin. "Well, it is uncomfortable. Especially because I see the way you look at me, and I don't appreciate it. I'm with someone now."

I don't know what comes over me, but it's hot and immediate. A knife slicing through my ribs. As Minnie describes his very public adoration, that same fire I used to get every time I heard Adam on a call with one of his girl-friends pulses through me. I hated when they pulled crap like this. Trying to pretend he was doing something wrong, like he was hitting on them, looking at them the wrong way, when he'd been the one to break up with them in the first place.

I'm not wearing a cocktail dress, nor do I have the perfect hair or makeup, but I throw my jacket at Rachel and march up to stand next to Justin. "Hey, there you are."

I have no idea what I'm doing, just that I can't stand the idea of him—of anyone—having to endure this alone.

I don't look at Minnie, don't even acknowledge her, just slip my arm around his waist and smile. Justin blinks, then, without a word, leans down and kisses me.

five

JUSTIN KISSES LIKE HE FLIRTS. Sure of himself. A little cocky. There's a clean, winter-cold edge to his mouth, like he was sucking on a mint. Is he still sucking on it? I swear something brushes past my lips, but I can't be sure it wasn't just the tip of his tongue. That thought sends a jolt to my thighs. Before I can think too hard about it, he's pulling away. My mouth follows his longer than it should, and I pull back only to find his hand on the small of my back, holding me in place.

And then I'm looking at him, thinking that if all pretend kisses were like that, we'd probably have a hell of a lot more real ones.

Minnie clears her throat, and I finally turn my head. She looks me up and down, and her smile tightens. "I didn't realize you had company."

Justin relaxes his grip so I can turn. "This is Sam."

"Hm." Minnie looks unimpressed. That only makes me smile bigger.

"Hi. And you are?"

Her eyes flare. "Minnie." She says it like "obviously" is

meant to be the trailer. But she doesn't know who she's messing with. I once pretended to be a lesbian so my roommate could make her boyfriend jealous.

My brows pinch just enough to say I have no idea why that name would be significant. "Nice to meet you. Are you here for the tournament?"

Rachel coughs, covering her mouth with her hand.

Minnie's nostrils flare. "Not for the Four Corners tournament if that's what you're asking. I have my own event at the Fieldhouse this weekend."

My eyes widen. "Oh! Well, that's great." I make it sound like I'm complimenting a kindergartner's first coloring project. It's a little much, but I'm having too much fun to stop myself.

Something flashes across her face. Annoyance. Disbelief. Hopefully both.

I sigh and lean into Justin. "Do you have to go back to the party? I'd love to head up. We've got an early morning."

Justin nods. "No, I made an appearance." His hand shifts from my lower back to take my hand. "Good seeing you, Minnie."

We walk past her before she can say anything else, and Rachel and Brooke fall into step next to us. Rachel flashes me a look of complete elation, but none of us says a word until we're safely closed into the elevator.

Then the four of us burst out laughing.

Justin drops my hand, and I reach for my coat that Rachel's still holding, wrapping my arms around it. Not because my hands are shaking and I feel like I just shotgunned a Red Bull or anything.

"Holy SHIT." Rachel explodes. "That was the best thing I've ever seen."

"Did you see her face?" Brooke gapes. "I can't believe you did that."

"And you!" Rachel grabs Justin's shoulder. "How dare you apologize! You didn't plan a tournament on top of hers!"

He groans. "I know. I didn't know what to say."

"How about f—" Rachel's cut off as the door opens and someone gets in on the second floor. She drops her hand, and we stand politely until the elevator reaches our floor. Then we walk like calm and refined adults to our room. But when the door shuts, we start right where we left off.

Rachel lets Justin have it. Talking about boundaries and self-respect. Brooke nods along with the occasional "Preach" hand lift.

I escape to the bathroom to get ready for bed so I don't end up brushing my teeth next to Justin, and when the door is locked, I deflate and lean over the sink.

I can't believe I did that.

My face is flushed in the mirror. Not in a bad way, more like . . . I look wholly alive.

I can't believe I did that.

The replay of that kiss is persistent, the taste of mint still on my lips. I splash water on my face and brush my teeth to erase the evidence. Then I realize I didn't bring my pajamas into the bathroom with me, and groan internally. It's fine. I'll wait until Justin's in his room and just change out there.

When I come back out, Rachel and Brooke are sprawled on the two living room chairs, still buzzing.

Brooke throws me an individually wrapped truffle.

I grin. "Okay if I save it till tomorrow? Just brushed my teeth." I scan the room for Justin. He's leaning against the counter, his back to us. Talking on the phone.

"Is he a good kisser?" Rachel hisses, and Justin turns his head.

"I heard that."

She chortles. "The question still stands."

I shrug. "I've had better."

Justin fully turns around at that. "I'm sorry, what?"

I breathe a sigh of relief. If we can joke about this, it won't feel awkward all weekend. "You heard me."

Justin murmurs something into the phone and drops it from his ear. "It's not a fair comparison. I was under pressure."

"Yeah, to make it look hot." Rachel swivels in the chair. "That should've been your best material."

"Well, it wasn't." He rounds the counter, and it's the first time I fully notice his outfit. He's in jeans and a nice sweater, the sleeves rolled halfway up his arms.

I shrug. "I can't speak to that. I have nothing to compare it to."

Justin moves like he's going to walk over and plant another one on me, and I hold up my hands. "No! It was great. Promise."

His jaw ticks, and then there's that easy smile. "Why is nobody asking me if Sam's a good kisser?"

Brooke makes a sound in her throat. "Because it's obvious."

The conversation devolves into whose job it is to be a good kisser on a first kiss, then on to whether or not it's possible to have a good kiss in public or whether it's all too performative.

When Brooke's eyes are fluttering closed, and she loses her thought mid-sentence, the three of them agree to call it a night.

I'm already tucked into bed, and Rachel hits the light as

they leave. It takes me about thirty seconds of closing my eyes to realize that, even though it's nearly eleven, I won't be able to fall asleep yet.

I text Alecia. When she doesn't respond immediately, I open my laptop and answer a few work emails. I'm amazed I haven't thought about work once since arriving at the hotel. It's only one evening, but still. That has to be a record. Especially considering the whole job opening announcement.

When I've solved the world's invitation problems, I flip on the TV and turn to the perma-*Friends* channel.

Perfect.

Until halfway through episode number two when a door opens. I flinch like I just got caught by my parents with a boyfriend.

Justin pads out of his room. Barefoot. Hoodie on, his hair still damp at the edges. He pauses when he sees me.

"I was worried I was going to wake you."

I shake my head. "Just winding down."

He wanders to the kitchen, grabs a glass of water, then meanders into the room. He stops next to the bed and locks onto the TV.

"This is the one where they find out Chandler and Monica are together."

"Yeah."

"Finally."

I laugh. "Finally."

We watch for what has to be almost ten minutes in silence, and I absorb nothing. I can't think with him standing so close.

"Was it really a bad kiss?" he says when the episode ends.

I look up at him with disbelief. "Is this what's keeping you up at night?"

"No, I just wondered—"

"It was a great kiss." That was the truth, and while I was all for joking before, I wasn't going to give the poor guy a complex. Though a little bit of humility probably wouldn't hurt in the long run.

His Adam's apple bobs. "Okay."

"Okay." I turn back to the TV, pretending to find a Shredded Mini Wheats commercial terribly engaging.

"But you know it wasn't my best, right? I thought it needed to seem like we'd done it before—"

I laugh out loud. "What do you think I'm going to do? Sign onto the Smash Point message board and rate you?"

He grins like the idea never occurred to him, but he wasn't opposed to it.

I drop back into my pillows with an exasperated sigh. "Don't you have to wake up early tomorrow?"

He nods.

"Then what are you doing standing here?" I shoo him back to his room, and Justin's smile widens.

"You're annoyed by me." He says it as a fact, not a question.

"No, I—"

"At the club, you always walk away when I'm talking."

"Because you're announcing tournaments. I don't play in tournaments."

"But most people still want to hear the info."

I give him a look. "I guess I'm not most people."

Justin looks like he's going to drop down and sit on the bed, so I splay out my hand on the mattress. "Go to bed, Justin."

Instead of getting my point across, he only looks more delighted. "Why don't you like me?"

"Right now? Because you won't leave me alone."

"No, in general."

I run my free hand over my face. "You have too much energy."

"Isn't that a good thing?"

"Not at midnight."

"In general, remember?"

I look up at him. "I'm sure it is. For most people."

His mouth quirks, and he looks at me for a long moment. "But you're not most people."

I swallow hard. "Right."

He considers this. "Okay."

I'm not sure why that was an acceptable answer, but I'll take it. "Goodnight, Justin."

He takes a few steps toward his room, reaching out to set his glass on the counter. Then he pauses and scratches his lower back, lifting his T-shirt to reveal a strip of skin.

Justin turns, but doesn't meet my eyes. "I appreciate what you did."

"Happy to help."

He looks up, and the smug smile is nowhere to be found. "I really appreciate it."

My ribs cinch. "I was worried you'd be pissed."

He huffs a breath. "No. Not pissed." He takes a backward step, pressing a hand into the doorframe. "Do you—?" He stops, tapping his finger against the wood. "I mean, would you pretend again? If we happen to be in the same place and Minnie's there?"

My pulse rushes in my ears. "Yeah. If you want me to."

He nods. "I don't need to prove anything to her."

"No, I know."

"But it's nice to not look like the loser for once."

I blink. Justin, with all the words I could use for him, is nowhere near loser territory. The fact that the word is in his head sends that flare to my ribs a second time.

Oh. Tomorrow, I am going to find a way for us to be in the same place as Minnie. And I will not be wearing my travel jeans.

I'm going to pretend the hell out of this.

six

BREAKFAST at the Summit Lodge smells like Christmas morning at my grandparents' house. Coffee, oranges, and bacon fat. I take a deep breath, surprised at the memories that wash over me.

I don't consider myself a terribly sentimental person, but my memories of my grandparents always get me. They died ten years ago. I don't take for granted these little pieces of them showing up in everyday life.

I fill up a plate and claim a corner of the long table, and Alecia drops into the chair across from me. "Okay. Start talking."

I tell her everything. Starting with how I walked into the apartment and found Justin there, shirtless. She drops her jaw and reacts at the right moments, but something about it feels off. Why do I get the feeling she isn't at all surprised Justin was in the room?

I ignore it and move on to the juicy bits. How Minnie cornered Justin, how I intervened.

This time, her gasp pulls a glance from a nearby table.

Alecia clamps a hand over her mouth, then grins like the Cheshire Cat. *"I can't believe you kissed him!"*

I scoop up a bite of eggs. "Technically, he kissed me."

"I just—" Alecia shakes her head. "I'm usually the one who pulls you into the crazy, and here you are doing it all by yourself."

"Are you so proud of me?"

"I really am."

She can tell I'm now invested in the Minnie drama, so we dive deep. I had no idea Calder and Justin were such good friends, or that Calder talked to anyone enough to have these kinds of details.

Alecia has all the tea. How Minnie kept him from talking to his family for over a year. How Justin lost fifteen pounds before he finally broke up with her.

I'm not a fan of woman-bashing, and relationships are never a one-way street, but it feels delicious to be a little self-indulgent.

When the conversation circles back to our kiss and late-night chat in the hotel room, I start to get antsy. I don't know why I'm avoiding those details—it isn't a big deal—but I feel the adrenaline shakes just thinking about it. Probably too much sugar from the chocolate muffin.

Alecia pulls up the day's schedule, and we see that Drew is playing singles first thing on Court Four. Quite a few people are playing from Smash Point today, and I hope to catch as many as I can. Alecia and I plan to rotate through the Fieldhouse, since Justin and Calder will be occupied most of the morning with orientations and logistics.

It's a quick walk across the street to the Fieldhouse. Inside, eighteen courts stretch under industrial roofing and huge circular lights, but somehow they've made the place feel cozy with a pro shop, a café, and lounge.

Alecia and I get in the short line for coffee, and it doesn't take me long to spot him. Justin walks the lanes between the first four courts, a walkie-talkie clipped to the waistband of his joggers, and a tablet in his hands. He pushes through the gate onto one of the courts and bends to adjust a net strap.

"Did you talk to him at all about Baseline Collective?" Alecia asks.

"His company, right?" I scan the area for banners or signs that would corroborate the name, but only find signage for Prestige Pickleball. Odd. Considering the situation, I'd think Justin would want everything about this tournament to be hyper visible.

I'm about to prod for more details on that question when the energy in the whole building shifts. Conversations hush. Heads turn.

Just inside the doors, Minnie strides past the registration area with Finn Johnson, both of them wearing Prestige athletic shirts. Her hand hooks into his elbow, and she laughs when he leans in to say something.

Finn smiles and waves as they move. A couple of players step forward, hands outstretched. He slows just enough to acknowledge them with a quick shake here, quick nod there, then keeps moving. He's polite and controlled as they angle toward the Prestige Pickleball table set up near the center courts.

It's covered with a black tablecloth, the branded banner overhead pulled tight. Two ring lights flank a DSLR on a tripod, and a social media person adjusts camera angles before waving them into the shot.

Minnie shifts closer to Finn, chin lifted, smile ready. The camera clicks.

I glance back at Justin. He's joking around with someone on Court Three. There are no lights, no staff members snapping pictures of him.

And that's when I get Alecia's question. Why she wasn't surprised to find out Justin was rooming with us. Hell, why she asked if I had any contacts who could use marketing advice.

"Alecia Monroe." I purse my lips and turn to face her. She's putting in her coffee order, so I have to wait a second for my indictment. When she looks up, I hiss, "You set this up."

seven

ALECIA WINCES. "I didn't set you up."

Oh, she was not going to play innocent on this one. "You absolutely did! You knew Justin was in the suite."

She lifts both hands. "I knew he *might* be."

"That's not any better."

Her mouth presses into a line. Then she sighs and leans her hip against the counter. "It wasn't like that."

"Like what?"

The staff member returns to the register, and I give my coffee order, then move to the side. Alecia steps closer. "Like . . . anything romantic. I just thought you needed a solo account. He needs marketing help. Badly."

I scoff. "And you couldn't tell me because?"

"Because every time I suggest you do something, you dig in your heels."

"I do not!" I motion to the scene around us. "Case in point!"

"Okay, but pickleball took some nudging."

"Pushing."

"Whatever, I'm just saying, you don't respond well to being forced into anything. It has to be your idea."

I give her a look.

"Unless it's for me, because you'll do anything for me because you love me," she amends. That was correct, no matter how much I complained about it.

"But this has to be for you, Sam." She turns and takes her coffee from the barista. "I just thought I could help you make the connection."

The barista calls my name next, and I take my cup. I draw a deep breath as we walk away from the counter.

I get she was trying to be helpful, but . . . "I don't want to get involved with someone I know in real life. A friend—Calder's friend. What if it doesn't go well? On either side?"

Alecia shrugs. "Justin's the most chill guy ever, are you kidding? Look how long it took him to break up with Minnie."

"No, that's even worse! He'll never say anything if he hates my work!"

Alecia nods immediately. "Totally fine. It was just an idea. And I'm sorry I didn't tell you."

I narrow my eyes. It's not often she gives in like that. No argument. "Alecia—"

"Hey! There's Calder!" she says.

Justin stands with Calder past the Prestige table on the opposite side of the aisle. He's in a Baseline Collective hoodie, so at least there's some branding. They both glance up at the same time.

Calder lifts his chin in greeting, and Justin . . .

His lips part, and he shifts on his feet. The movement is subtle, but my brain latches onto it, sending a rush of energy down my spine.

I'm instantly self-conscious, thinking about the extra

time I took this morning blowing out my hair. The concealer and mascara I don't normally bother with on the weekends. I went back and forth between two outfits, then settled on my tight black leggings, a tank top, and my oversized gray crop zip-up.

I didn't do this for him. But I'd be lying if I said I didn't do it for someone who just happened to be flaunting herself next to the Prestige table.

Minnie's watching us. Her gaze is like a pair of twin lasers burning into the back of my neck. So I don't slow or hesitate. I walk straight up to Justin, set my coffee down on the edge of the table next to him, wrap my arms around his neck, and plant a quick peck on his lips.

His skin is warm, his cheek a little scratchy with stubble. He wears a subtle scent that I've never noticed before being this close to him. Twice.

Justin's smile stalls for half a second, surprise flickering through it, before it widens. His hand comes to my waist without thinking, his fingers brushing the strip of bare skin between my waistband and the hem of my shirt.

"Morning," he says.

"Morning," I reply.

Behind us, Alecia makes a sound that could be a laugh of surprise or a straight-up inhale of her coffee.

* * *

There might not be any proof that time travel exists, but watching pickleball games at least makes time warp. One moment, Alecia and I are talking with Calder and Justin. I am, admittedly, very flirty, and the next thing I know, it's three o'clock, and we're watching Rachel fight through her 4.0 singles bracket.

Alecia and I stand at the rail with the remnants of our wraps we bought at the café around two when we realized our stomachs were eating themselves.

Rachel hits a crazy shot down the line to take third place, and she walks off the court elated. Brooke loops an arm around her shoulders, and I can't wait to watch them play doubles in the morning. All in all, Smash Point players made four of the eight singles podiums, which is damn impressive.

After snapping pictures of Rachel with her medal, Alecia and I wait near the café using one of Alecia's old Garrett notepads to mark the number of times Minnie waits to burst out laughing until Justin is within earshot.

"She has to know how obvious that is," Alecia murmurs.

Minnie presses a hand to Finn's chest like she's posing for a lifestyle stock photo shoot. Justin and Calder walk by with a basket of balls, neither of them seeming to notice. But the fact that they don't look up at all tells me it's purposeful.

Prestige has full-on sashes, pomp, and circumstance for their winners, but when I look over at the nine Baseline courts, they're still full of people. Competitors are standing on the courts and in the aisles, laughing and chatting. It takes Justin at least ten minutes to make it to us because he keeps getting pulled into conversations.

My brain starts to spin. His branding should be the exact opposite of Prestige. Colorful. Warm. A font that's inviting. Professional, but cozy. The whole thing should be community. Comfortable. What's that trending Danish vibe? Hygge.

" . . . I think that will just be easier, you know?"

I blink. Alecia was talking to me, but I have no idea

what she said. "Yeah. For sure." Zero clue what I just agreed to.

"Great. It's settled." She grins as Justin and Calder finally approach, bags slung over their shoulders. "Sam and I think we should do the hotel restaurant for dinner. Sound good?"

I breathe a silent sigh of relief that it was only dinner and not doing the Manitou Incline or something equally heinous.

We walk back to the hotel to find the restaurant is as busy as it was on the first night. Thankfully, Calder was bright enough to call over and put us on the wait list. It's only fifteen minutes before we're at a table. When the server arrives, Calder barely has to look at the menu. "Grilled chicken sandwich. Extra pickles."

Alecia flips the pages. "Truffle fries for the table and . . . the Gyro for me."

Justin rests his arm on the table and looks up at our server with what I used to call his sales smile. Now I'm wondering if it's just his normal face. "What's your favorite thing on the menu?"

Our server, a cute blond with a girl-next-door look, lights up. "Our burger's fantastic. Grass-fed, locally—"

"You had me at burger," he says. "Medium. Add bacon."

She beams. "Excellent choice. And to drink?"

"Whatever local beer is your favorite."

Her cheeks flush, and taking my order is an afterthought. I don't think she takes her eyes off Justin when she types in my Reuben.

She walks away, and I reach for my water, giving Alecia a look. She laughs, and Justin looks between the two of us.

"What?"

Calder sniffs. "I'm guessing it has something to do with the way you just glazed our waitress."

Justin laughs. "What? I asked her opinion—"

"And you just take it?" I say. "What if she recommended liver and onions?"

"Then I would've ordered it," he says.

I scoff. "Just shovel it down if you hate it?"

Justin laughs. "I wouldn't hate it."

"That's true," Calder says. "He likes everything."

I give him a look. That wasn't possible. He had to have opinions and was just a people pleaser. I wasn't going to argue that point, but I wanted to.

"Well, regardless, you made love to her with that order," I say, and Alecia nearly spits out her water.

He holds out his hands like he has no idea what we're talking about.

"Seriously?" I shift in my chair, preparing for a full dressing-down. "What do women want more than anything, Justin?"

"Dresses with pockets?" Calder murmurs, and Alecia smacks his shoulder.

Justin shrugs. "A six pack."

"Uh, false," I say.

Alecia slips a hand under Calder's shirt. "I mean, it doesn't hurt."

Calder shivers.

I roll my eyes. "They want to be seen. Listened to. What you just did? Smiling, asking her opinion, then doing whatever she told you? That was foreplay."

He throws an arm over the back of his chair, and his leg juts out, bumping mine. He doesn't move it. "It is not. I was just being nice."

That knee against mine? Foreplay. I can't tell if he's now egging me on.

I motion to his entire being. "This? It's an act, right? You can't be that oblivious."

"No, he's that oblivious," Calder says.

"You have to see how women fawn over you." I glance around the room. "How many of the people from Smash Point who signed up for this tournament are women?"

He opens his mouth, then closes it. "I don't know. Maybe half?"

Alecia starts counting them off, and when we get to fifteen people with an eighty-percent female ratio, he waves us off.

"That isn't because of me."

Our fries arrive, and I grab two, dipping them in the garlic aioli. I don't have to make a rebuttal. He can stew on that and come to his own conclusions.

"I don't accept this line of reasoning," Justin says. "Because if I was that good at attracting women, I wouldn't be sleeping alone in my hotel room."

I level my gaze at him. "You're *sleeping* with three women."

That gets a guttural laugh out of Calder, and I rest my case.

He did make a good point, though. Attracting the opposite sex and actually landing in a relationship are two different things. Totally different skill sets. I'm pondering that when Brooke and Rachel appear at our table, just as our food is being delivered. As if our prior conversation conjured them out of thin air.

Rachel covers Justin's ears. "Don't rat us out to the boss, but we're going to a bar downtown. Just a couple of drinks."

Justin grabs her wrists and pulls her hands away. "What was that? Are you being irresponsible? Giving Baseline a bad name?"

Rachel laughs. "Try a *good* name. Brooke's not wearing a bra."

Brooke does a little shimmy, and Justin pretends he's pulling dollar bills from his underwear.

You really can't make this shit up.

Justin picks up his burger. "Text me the address. I just need to eat and change." He turns to the rest of us. "You in?"

I meet Alecia's eyes, sending a telepathic, *if I'm not tucked into bed in an hour, someone's getting kicked in the balls.*

She fights a smile. "I think we're going to turn in."

"Code for we're having sex, perrrrfect," Rachel says. "Not jealous at all."

Calder smirks, throwing an arm over Alecia's shoulders.

I sigh. "And I'm . . . not having sex. I'm just boring and want to go to bed."

Brooke laughs and steals a fry. "I'm a little bit jealous of that, though."

Rachel looks scandalized. "What?! This was your idea!"

They argue their way into the lobby while we start in on our meal. The food is excellent, simple and exactly what you want from bar food. When I finish, my fingers are covered with grease and salt.

Justin and I walk back to the room together, and I count three yawns from him by the time we reach our door.

"You seem totally ready to party." I swipe my key card and push the door open.

"It was all that foreplay. I'm tuckered out."

I roll my eyes. "It's hard work being that desirable."

"I'm sure you would know."

I snort. "Mmhm. Right."

He frowns as I slip off my shoes. "I wasn't joking."

I make a sound in my throat. "Okay."

I start toward the living room, but Justin grabs my elbow, spinning me back toward him. Then he does his best Sam impression. "You can't be this oblivious."

I open my mouth, then close it. I have no idea what's happening right now.

"You're drop-dead gorgeous."

I throw my eyes to the ceiling, uncomfortable with the aggressive amount of eye contact and, you know, compliments. "If only my personality was as good as my ass."

Justin huffs a laugh. "Stop it."

I take a step back and give a fake bow, then walk to my sofa bed. Justin putters around the kitchen, which is inconvenient because I have nothing to do but change or go into his bathroom. Neither of which I want to do in his presence.

"Aren't you going to change and head out?" I ask.

He yawns again. "Yep. Just grabbing an energy drink."

I turn, my tank top and shorts in hand. "You can say no, you know. That's an option."

He looks at me like I'm speaking a foreign language.

I set my clothes on the chair and walk into the kitchen. He steps back as I open the cupboard next to him and pull out a bag of microwave popcorn from Brooke's stash.

I hold it out, then make a show of ripping the plastic open with my teeth. "I'm going to sit in my warm bed and watch *Friends*. And eat popcorn."

He laughs. "I'm listening."

"I'm going to wash my face and moisturize and put on cozy socks—"

Justin leans closer, and my heart skips a beat. His eyes drop to my mouth, then back up. "And you say I'm good at foreplay."

I blurt an awkward laugh and almost fall over as I turn to the microwave. That was on purpose. Definitely.

Even though I know he's messing with me, I like it. I like when he pays attention to me. I like that he told me I'm gorgeous. I'm aware that I'm a reasonably attractive woman, but I was serious about the personality thing.

Men like bubbly. Fun, outgoing. Men like girls like Alecia.

I set the popcorn on the glass turntable and close the door to the microwave, suddenly unable to read English and find where the popcorn setting is.

Justin reaches over my shoulder and presses the button. The microwave whirs to life.

When I turn to face him, he's looking down at his phone, tapping away with his thumbs. "I think . . . that something I ate at dinner isn't agreeing with me."

I frown. "Really? Was it the pink in the burger? Because—"

He grins and turns his phone to face me. It's a text. To Brooke and Rachel.

Oh. I swallow hard. "You're not going out."

He presses send, then slips the phone in his pocket. "I'll go get my socks."

I DON'T KNOW why we sit on my sofa bed instead of his king, but we do. My parents would be proud. There's more than two Bibles worth of space between the two of us.

Friends isn't on, but *Seinfeld* is. I can't tell which show I love more.

"You're hogging the popcorn." Justin reaches for the bowl.

I laugh. "I've barely had one handful."

Onscreen, Jerry refuses to kiss people hello as a matter of morality, and Justin pounces. "See, this is what I'm saying. Forced kisses are always bad kisses."

I smirk. "You're still stuck on that?"

He grabs popcorn and motions to the television. "I haven't been thinking about it. It's just relevant."

Elaine rants about social obligation, about who deserves a kiss and who doesn't. Whether it means something or not.

"What do you think?" Justin asks.

"Who deserves a kiss?"

He shakes his head. "No. When it means something."

"Doesn't it always mean something?" I say. He raises an eyebrow, and I backtrack. "No, not when it's a joke. I just mean, in general."

"Maybe not." He considers this, then turns toward me, resting on his elbow. "Did you ever practice kissing with your pillow?"

I bark a laugh. "My pillow? No. Can't say I did."

"Cool. Me neither." He starts to roll back, but I stop him.

"Okay, I didn't practice with my pillow, but I did . . . with my hand." I shouldn't have admitted it. The smug look on his face means his ego just grew two sizes.

"See? What if it didn't have to mean anything? If we could practice with other people?"

"Pretty sure I was eight when I made out with my palm."

He chuckles. "Were you, though?"

I smack him.

He leans back on the pillows, resting his arm behind his head. "What if it was just curiosity. Or informational gathering. Like, asking if some technique was good or not."

"But wouldn't the response be different for everyone?"

"I think a good kiss is a good kiss."

I shake my head. "No. Some people like weird stuff."

"True. But there are certain things that everyone likes."

I give him a look. "Really. You sound pretty sure of yourself."

"I am."

I pull my legs up under me in a criss-cross. "A good kiss has to be created. There has to be feedback—"

"Oh, there's definitely feedback. But that doesn't mean it can't happen straight out of the gates."

"But it depends on the moment. The comfort level, trust. Hormone levels."

He nods, his hand shifting on the blanket. His hand is an inch away from mine, not that I'm paying attention.

"You can talk all you want."

"But?"

He glances over. "I know I'm right."

I chortle. "Of course you do."

We watch the show for a few more minutes, but the audio may as well have been Charlie Brown's teacher. Nothing is computing, in or out.

"I think I should show you," Justin says finally, pushing up to sit.

"Show me what?"

"My best kiss."

My breath hitches. *My best kiss?* What was I supposed to say to that? My curiosity silences any other thought in my head, and I nod.

Justin swallows. Then he shifts, close enough that my knee brushes his, and the heat from his body makes my skin prick. He lifts a hand like he's going to tuck my hair back, then pauses. He scans my face, and my cheeks heat.

"This part matters," he says.

"Hm?"

"The anticipation."

I nod again.

His thumb settles against my jaw. "My best kisses don't start with kissing."

"Right." My voice is thin.

He smiles, slow and crooked. "Our heads are so full that it takes a minute to be present."

Oh, I am very present. I don't remember my life before Justin's hand was touching my cheek. I don't think I'm aware of any of my extending limbs, actually.

He lowers his head, and his breath brushes against my

lips first. My pulse bucks. Then his mouth brushes mine, and he pulls back a fraction, his eyes on my mouth.

And I realize, possibly for the first time, that what turns me on about kissing is seeing him enjoy it. Want it. Anticipate it. It's like my feelings, my enjoyment, every sensation, is doubled by watching him experience it along with me.

I'm not going to keep my eyes open the whole time—I'm not a serial killer—but this part, the beginning, I want to witness.

Justin fits his mouth to mine, unhurried, and my hand curls into his shirt.

"Good," he breathes, and heat flashes through my body. Uh, I like that. I like that a lot.

His mouth moves with intention now, breathing me in, his hand slipping around the back of my neck. When my lips part, he slides into the space I make.

"This is where people mess it up," he whispers. "They rush." He kisses the corner of my mouth. Then my lower lip. Then he presses his forehead to mine, forcing me to listen to our breath.

"That's how I can tell." His hand presses into my lower back.

"Tell what?" I pant, realizing my back is arched, that I'm pressing into him.

"That you want more." He kisses me again, easing me back on the pillows, his chest rolling over mine.

I barely register the sound of the door clicking, but when I hear Brooke's laugh, my whole body snaps to attention.

Justin flies off me, sitting bolt upright and pulling a pillow onto his lap. I scramble up to sit next to him. We look like two Barbie dolls with how rigid our spines are.

When I turn my head, Brooke and Rachel stand in the doorway like two deer caught in a floodlight.

"Hey!" Justin blurts. "You're back early."

They look between the two of us, their eyes narrowing.

Rachel says, "And you don't look sick."

He runs a hand over his face. "Yeah. Still not a hundred percent, but I couldn't sleep, so we were watching TV."

"Uh-huh." Brooke smirks. "What's happening in the episode?"

"It's the one where Jerry and Elaine argue about who they should greet with a kiss." The sentence comes out of me like a single word in German. No pauses.

Rachel purses her lips. "Interesting."

Justin, bless his heart, gets them talking about their night at the bar. It was great despite the early return, but they were serious about getting good sleep before competing in doubles the next day.

I have no idea if they saw anything. Positive they suspected, but I doubt they had proof that anything happened between us. I don't know why I care, but I do.

That was hands down the best kiss of my life, and honestly, what clinched it was being interrupted. It was like being dragged up out of a lake by my hair. Now I was wet and cold and disappointed, and all I wanted to do was launch myself back in.

I rush to the bathroom to start my bedtime routine while they're still talking, and when Justin walks in thirty seconds later, I jolt.

I just splashed water on my face. "Sorry, do you need—"

He shakes his head. "No, finish up, it's fine." He reaches for his toothbrush, and I squeeze a dollop of face wash into my palm. I wash quickly, then grab my microfiber face towel to dry. When I surface, Justin's looking at his phone screen with a scowl.

"You good?" I ask, somehow succeeding in blocking the last half hour from my brain so I don't press him up against the door and ask him to start where we left off.

He sighs. "Yeah. It's not good for me to check socials right now."

I reach for my toothbrush, my mind instantly going to Minnie. I don't want to make assumptions, so I say, "Bad news?"

Justin grabs his toothbrush and toothpaste. "Prestige posted fifteen times today, I think. With their setup." He shakes his head. "It looks really good."

Meaning his doesn't.

My conversation with Alecia jumps back into my head, and before I can access all the reasons why I shouldn't bring this up with Justin, my brain latches on to the possibility that I might get more of what happened on the sofa bed if I have a reason to spend more time with him.

"You know I do marketing for a living, right?" I say.

Justin's toothbrush freezes halfway to his mouth. "You do? I thought you worked for a paper company."

I nod. "Pixel and Paper. The company started off doing invitations and special event printing, but we now offer full branding consultations and marketing packages." The irony of this conversation is not lost on me. Considering how much I internally mocked Justin for being too sales-y.

He turns and leans against the counter. "That would be . . . yeah. I need something like that. I probably need to hire on more staff, too."

"Who do you have working for you?"

"Just a virtual assistant."

My eyes widen. "Seriously?" I think back to the tournament today. Managing the registrations and courts, not to mention the behind-the-scenes work with the venue and online advertising. He has to be doing online advertising, right?

"Do you run ads for these tournaments?"

Justin shakes his head. "No, we just post about it with affiliated clubs."

"Are you serious?"

He looks up, all wide-eyed and innocent. "Yeah, is that bad?"

Justin, Justin, Justin. Here he was standing in a bathroom scrolling through socials for Prestige—a company that probably spent thousands each month on marketing pushes—comparing himself when he had one VA and a few social media posts.

He runs a hand through his hair. "I have a budget for it, I just don't know where to start—"

"How much is your budget?"

He shrugs. "I'd have to check, but I have around forty thousand dollars set aside to get some stuff made—"

"Forty grand?"

"Yeah. Not enough?"

"No, that's plenty." My heart starts to race. "Full transparency, I want to apply for a promotion at work. I need a solo account, a project I can submit. So what I'm about to say comes with a high personal bias—"

"I want you," Justin says.

My pulse kicks. *I want you.* The words flash in my head, and I blink. Right. For the marketing. That's obviously what he was talking about.

I clear my throat. "I haven't given you my fees yet."

"I don't care. I want you to do it."

I huff a laugh. "That's not good business. I could say whatever I want—"

"I trust you. Just tell me what you need from me."

"But you haven't seen my work. You don't even know—"

"Are you trying to talk me out of this?" He grins.

"No! But what if you don't like it—"

"I will." His smile widens, and I remember the conversation at dinner.

"No." I run my toothbrush under the water.

"No, what?"

"No, like I don't think this is a good idea."

"You're the one who brought it up!"

"I—" I fold my arms across my chest, forgetting about my toothbrush and nearly smearing my left bicep with toothpaste. I set it on the counter. "I can't create a marketing plan and then have you hate it and not tell me."

"I won't hate it."

"Yeah, I know that's what you say, but . . . " My eyes land on the hand cream, and my chest tightens. Adam didn't hate anything either.

"Fine. I'll make you a deal."

I look up.

"I'll tell you everything," he says. When I don't respond, he continues, "Every thought in my head. You'll hear it all. Then you won't have to wonder."

My throat thickens, and I reach for my toothbrush to distract myself. "And you'll fire me? If it doesn't work out?"

Justin wets his lips. "Based on this conversation, I'm pretty sure I wouldn't have to. You'd just fire yourself."

nine

THE LAST RALLY dies in the air like a soap bubble. A snap followed by that split-second hush, and then the Fieldhouse detonates into applause.

Next to me, Alecia holds her breath. "That sucks. So dang close."

Rachel drops her paddle hand to her thigh, then Brooke attacks her from behind with a hug. I race with Alecia to the side of the fence closest to them, and they walk over.

"Two points!" Rachel groans.

They just missed the podium in doubles. Fourth. The worst possible number if you're competitive.

"It was an incredible match," Alecia says. It isn't just a comfort line. Their athleticism and patience blew me away.

We flit across the aisle to watch Drew and his partner finish their final. The last point is a clean put-away by Drew. Straight to their opponents' feet at a wicked angle.

We cheer and congratulate, then snap plenty of pictures when they get their medals from Justin.

A single VA. I'm blown away that he's been able to

accomplish all this on his own, and I'm dying to get back to the room and start working on some mock-ups. But it's not just the marketing I'm obsessing over. He needs systems. Automations. Work flows and SOPs. I have a thousand things I want to go through with him to make sure he's got good infrastructure for scale.

Stay in your lane, Sam. I mentally berate myself. This isn't my business. I don't have any right to jump in and tell him how to run it. But just like I stepped up next to him when Minnie was in the hall, I feel this strange pull to jump in and help with this.

Red flag, A. Isn't that what I've always told Alecia when she felt the need to be what people wanted?

But this isn't what Justin wants, is it? This is something else entirely. Boredom? Control issues? I know it isn't about the promotion at work anymore because if Alecia didn't keep reminding me about it, I doubt I would've taken any action because of that email.

It's what I should want on paper. But why am I more excited by the idea of managing Justin's business than moving up at Paper and Pixel?

Control issues. Has to be that.

After the final podium pics, we find Justin near the sideline where the event staff is already starting to stack chairs. Prestige is breaking down, too. Good timing for all of us.

Justin sees me coming, and his face lights up. "Hey."

It's like my chest is a Coke bottle and that one word dropped a Menthos into it. I'm fizzing with energy, and I don't know what to do with it.

"Hey," I say, then redirect my path to start hauling chairs with everyone else.

Justin starts, "You don't have to—!"

"I want to!" I call back over my shoulder.

It isn't until I head back for my second load that I notice what's happening on Court Three. Cheers lift, and there's a big crowd in the aisles.

Finn Johnson steps onto the featured court in his sponsored athletic wear and taps paddles with another woman I recognize. Amy Lee Lake.

I frown in confusion. She already did an exhibition game for Baseline Collective, so why is she on the court with Finn?

Someone yanks the chair from my hands, and I yelp.

Justin puts a hand on my shoulder. "Go watch. I'll take care of this."

"But—"

He turns me around and gives me a little nudge.

I'm too intrigued to argue, so I wander over and stand next to Drew, Brooke, and Rachel. "What's going on?"

Rachel shrugs. "They're playing singles. For fun, I think."

This definitely wasn't announced, and everyone is still breaking down around us. It gives me a thrill to think that these two pickleball celebrities would love the sport enough to challenge each other off the record.

The game starts and Finn's crazy fast without looking rushed in the least. His paddle grip looks almost lazy, and his strides and shuffles are smooth and consistent.

Amy Lee looks like a coiled spring. She bounces on the toes of her feet, watching the ball like a hungry coyote, ready to snap at the first sign of weakness.

Finn flicks a forehand roll that kisses the sideline, and I don't see how Amy could ever get back in time. And yet she does.

The crowd oohs. Someone whistles.

"If I could play with even half that energy . . ." Drew says beside me, and I nod my head in agreement.

The hairs on the back of my neck prickle, and I turn to see Justin talking with a staff member and—

Oh shit. Incoming.

Minnie's marching down the aisle. Straight toward him.

ten

MINNIE MOVES through people like she's entitled to more space than the rest of us commoners. Her hair is glossy and straight, her outfit perfectly tailored.

She heads straight for Justin, and I calculate how I can get to him without making it look like I followed her.

Chairs. They're still moving chairs.

A staff member is carrying a box to the back court, and I intercept her. "Can I take that for you?"

She blinks. "Sure. We need it at Court Nine."

"Got it." I take it from her hands and rush back there just in time to hear Minnie say, "Wow. Big day, huh?"

Justin smiles, but I've started noticing the differences in his expressions. His lips might curve right now, but there's no light in his eyes. No spark.

He shoves his hands in his pockets. "Oh, Minnie, hey."

"How did it go?" She asks like Amy Lee plays pickleball. Hunting for weakness.

"Really well," he answers. "A lot of happy people."

Minnie laughs. "Sure."

I drop the box next to the court with more flair than

necessary, and when Minnie looks over, I pop up and walk toward them. "Oh, hi! Macey, right?"

Her nostrils flare. "Minnie."

"Right! So sorry. Lots of names to learn this weekend." I sidle up to Justin, and he pulls his hand from his pocket. I take it.

Her face pinches. "And you are . . . ?"

I fight a laugh. *Great move, Minnie. Super original.* "Sam," I say with a bright smile.

Justin's thumb strokes once over my knuckle. "What about Prestige? Happy with the results?"

Minnie doesn't miss that he asked about her company, not her specifically. "Great. Yeah, really great." She flicks her hair over her shoulder. "It's just brave, you know? To take on something this big when you're already so stretched."

Justin frowns. "Not sure what you mean."

"Oh, I just mean that at Prestige you were always so stressed. Like, life is pretty stressful for you, so then to add running a business."

Justin's jaw ticks, and her eyes flare. She knows she hit a nerve.

I've never wanted to slap someone in the face so badly.

Justin must feel me tense because he drops my hand and pulls me close to his side. "No, working at Prestige was stressful, but this has been a good move."

Minnie starts blathering on about some other way Justin's failing, but I can't hear her through my red, hot rage. How dare she say this shit? Even if Justin did suck at life, why would you rub his face in it?

And that's when it clicks. Finn, her boyfriend, is playing a pickleball game right now, and where is Minnie?

Minnie isn't happy with Finn. She wants Justin, and she just has a screwed up way of trying to accomplish that.

"I'm sorry," I cut in. "It seems like you two have some catching up to do, so I'm going to get back to work." I reach a hand up and pull Justin's face to mine. I kiss him, slow and sweet, hoping he gets the message.

When I walk away, I know Minnie does.

What's the tightest nerve I could hit? That I'm so confident in our relationship, in myself, in him as a person living his damn life, that I'm happy to leave him alone with her.

I grin as I turn my back and walk away to pick up more chairs.

eleven

THE DRIVE back from the Fieldhouse feels longer than it should.

Alecia's wedged into the passenger seat, shoes kicked off, knees tucked up, and feet on the dash. I'm scrolling like a mad woman, hotspotting on my phone, creating a vision board for Baseline Collective. Alecia briefly tried to strike up a conversation, but she knows how I get when I'm into a project. Since I admitted it was work for Baseline, she hasn't said another damn word.

By the time we re-enter the Denver city limits, I've sent an email to Justin with my fee structure, discounted purely because this is my first solo, and a proposed plan of action with alternative timelines.

I feel wholly accomplished when Calder drops me off at my apartment. We say our goodbyes-for-now, and I walk into the brick building.

The interior of my apartment looks the same as always. I give a silent cheer when I flick the light switch and see the power's back on. Hallelujah.

I drop my bag by the door and stand there. I usually

love the quiet, but after staying with Rachel, Brooke, and Justin, it feels a little empty.

I kick off my shoes and pad into the kitchen, then jump when my phone buzzes.

RACHEL:

> FOURTH PLACE REVENGE TOUR. Smash
> Point. Tomorrow, 6pm?

BROOKE:

> Sam, you're drilling with us. We're going to
> get your DUPR up to 3.5

I smile, a little giddy. It's like I'm in middle school again and someone invited me to their party.

ME:

> I accept your terms and conditions

Am I free tomorrow after work? Probably. Alecia and I don't have firm plans until Wednesday dinner. I check my calendar to confirm, then toss my phone onto the couch and change into sweats.

I'm brushing my teeth, surprised at how disappointing

it feels to be doing that by myself, when my phone buzzes again.

Justin.

We exchanged numbers to talk marketing before we left the hotel. I pause before opening the message, wondering if he's getting ready for bed, too.

JUSTIN:

> You home safe?

I stare at the screen, toothbrush paused mid-foam. *A very non-professional question.* My heart speeds.

ME:

> Yep. Got in about an hour ago. You?

Three dots appear. Disappear. Appear again.

JUSTIN:

> Just arrived

He barely got home, and the first thing he did was text me?

Justin:

> Thanks for today

He's probably talking about that thing with Minnie, but I type:

> I did carry a lot of chairs

I spit and rinse my mouth and toothbrush, then set it back on its holder and turn to lean against the counter.

Justin:

> Actually why I'm texting. Need your Venmo
> to send the staff daily rate

I snort.

Me:

Phew. I thought this was going to be
awkward

JUSTIN:

You heading to bed?

My heart clicks into a new gear, and I'm instantly back on
that sofa bed. Kissing him. We never had a chance to talk
about that. Part of me wonders if it even happened, considering Brooke and Rachel haven't said a thing, either.

ME:

Soon. So tired. You?

JUSTIN:

I have to eat first

I hope you have a few waitresses on call. To
give you recommendations

I'm all foreplayed out

I laugh out loud.

ME:

Not possible

JUSTIN:

We should get together this week. To talk
business

You jump from foreplay to that?

Obviously

Lol. How about Friday?

I'm going to be catching up the next couple of days, and I already have a few client meetings scheduled on Wednesday and Thursday. I don't want to wait until the end of the week to see Justin. But that's the reality of it.

JUSTIN:

Might be tough. I'll be in ABQ

I frown, and then that piece of info clicks into place. The tournament. It's called Four Corners because it's traveling to all four corner states in four weekends.

Well, crap.

M E:

> When do you leave?

JUSTIN:

Friday morning

> Perfect timing

Is that your only free day?

I scroll to my calendar and search for any other opening that would work for a new client. I need at least a few hours with him to workshop some of these ideas.

M E:

> Unfortunately. I think it is

JUSTIN:

> Could we talk on the drive? I saw your
> email, and I'm in for all of that

Shocking. Considering he didn't even care to see the cost before signing up in the hotel room.

ME:

> That would definitely work. I could send you
> some ideas after we talk. Stay connected
> over the weekend?

JUSTIN:

> Would love that

Another skip of my pulse. Because he's excited to get the marketing going.

I think through this new plan. If he gets back Sunday night, we could— I groan, looking at my calendar. Next week is the repositioning sprint for Highline. Dammit. I'm the interim creative lead, which means daily standups and executive reviews. It's a big opportunity, and I should be excited. *Why am I pulling back from these career milestones I've worked so hard to achieve?*

. . .

ME:

> Trying to find time to connect once you're
> back. Didn't remember how busy the new
> year was going to be

Ideally, we'd be pushing this along as fast as the repositioning sprint. I don't want Justin to have to wait a month to implement new branding, especially when he has built-in opportunities to roll it out.

ME:

> Looks like Friday again next week, but
> you're probably traveling again

JUSTIN:

> I am. Arizona. What does your weekend
> look like?

ME:

> It's open, but I'd love to be in person for the
> design and logo finalizations
>
> It's so much easier to nail things down

JUSTIN:

> Makes sense
>
> So . . . what if you came with?

I slip on the counter and almost fall onto the toilet. *What if you came with?* Where? To Arizona?

JUSTIN:

> If you want. Paid because you're contracting with Baseline
>
> I won't even make you haul chairs
>
> But I know you will anyway

I work to force my rational brain to come online.

ME:

> To be clear, you're talking about the tournament in Arizona?

JUSTIN:

> Correct. Flying to Phoenix Friday at 11am, home Sunday at 9pm

. . .

Would I be sharing a room with him again? No . . . but maybe? Was he staying with other people? Was—

My thumbs start tapping.

ME:

Will Minnie be there?

The dots appear. Disappear.

JUSTIN:

Yes

Ah. Is that why he wants me to come? To continue the ruse? Before I can type a response, my phone rings.

"Hey," I answer.

"That's not why I want you to come. You don't have to—"

"No, Justin, it's fine. I'm happy to be your fake tournament girlfriend."

He lets out a heavy breath. "That's not why I asked."

I nod. "Okay."

"I'm serious."

"Okay, I get it."

"You said in person, and I thought it would give us more time to talk about all the marketing. And stuff."

I try not to overanalyze the pause before "and stuff" but it's impossible. "Yeah, no, that makes sense. Would we fly together?"

He laughs. "Yes, Sam. I wouldn't make you get your own ticket. Paid, remember?"

"That eats into your budget."

"Will you stop trying to tell me you're not worth it?"

I suck in a breath. That wasn't what I was saying, was it? Did I believe I wasn't good enough for a company to want to pay for me to attend their event?

Or was I worried this looked a lot like Minnie. Taking advantage of Justin's generosity for my own gain?

He pauses for a beat, then exhales. "Sorry, that's a lot to ask. I feel like I'm the only one benefiting from this situation."

I almost laugh out loud. And here I thought I was taking advantage of him. "Well, you are paying me."

I can hear the smile in his voice when he says, "For which part?"

I laugh. "Nice."

"If you have a girlfriend pay structure—"

"Okay. Goodnight, Justin."

"Wait! Don't hang up."

I pause in the doorway to my bedroom. We stand there in silence a moment. There's a rustle of fabric, the rush of his breath.

"Do you want to watch something?" he asks.

"Like . . ."

"Just on the phone," he hurries to clarify. "We turn it on at the same time."

My heart swells like a water balloon attached to a hose. I walk to the bed and climb on, searching for my Fire TV Stick remote. "Okay. We could do that."

twelve

ALECIA'S at my desk when I arrive at work Monday morning, a little bleary-eyed because Justin and I stayed up until one watching the new *Mission Impossible*. We couldn't have picked a better movie for late-night commentary, truly.

"You look . . . great." Alecia raises an eyebrow.

"Don't even." I pick up the coffee she made for me in the break room and take a sip. "Thank you."

"No prob. Up late?" she asks. I shuffle some papers on my desk, trying to come up with a response, when Alecia blurts, "I know you were talking to Justin! Calder told me."

My eyes fly wide. "What? How often do they talk?"

"They were supposed to do early morning pickleball, but Justin bailed. Said he was up late talking to you."

I drop into my chair.

"Well?" She taps her fingers on her arm.

I can't fight my smile for a second longer. "We watched a movie together."

"Over the phone?" she whispers, even though five seconds ago she was practically yelling, and my door is shut. Alecia pulls my egg chair closer to the desk and plops down.

I fill her in. It's nothing too exciting until I get to the part where I'm going to Arizona with him next weekend.

Alecia stares at me, and I wonder if someone just pressed pause on our conversation. "What?" She finally reanimates.

"Yeah, he thought that would give us time to work through some of—"

"Are you staying with him?"

I shrug. "Not sure. I need to ask him about that." Since Minnie will be there, I'm guessing we'll be in the same room. Maybe a suite again?

Alecia's lips purse. "Are you okay with this?"

"Yeah. Since he's going to be gone—"

"No." She pops up from the chair and rounds the desk, then takes my hands in hers. "Are you *okay* with this?"

My mouth opens and closes like a fish.

Alecia continues, "You did an amazing thing for him this weekend, helping him with Minnie. But—" She pauses. "Justin's a great guy. He's also . . . "

"A little like you?" I supply.

She nods emphatically. "Exactly. He jumps into things and doesn't always think about the consequences. And I think there might be consequences. For you. You know, if you keep pretending and . . . sleeping with him."

I chortle. "I'm not sleeping with him!"

"Yet." Her face scrunches.

I squeeze her hand. "This is very meta. You talking about not thinking about consequences while thinking about consequences."

She nods. "Maybe I'm only capable of doing that for you?"

Alecia is usually all gas, and I'm supposed to be the one tapping the brakes. It's like we went to Colorado Springs and came back in an alternate universe. "This is very unfamiliar territory."

"I know. It feels wrong." She thinks for a moment, then straightens and clears her throat. "I'm okay with you going next weekend, but you need to communicate clearly so I know what's happening and who you're with. Also, make good choices. And remember who you are."

My grin splits my face. "Got it."

She drops my hands and stands. "I'm probably overreacting. You've only ever kissed in public, so it's not like—" She freezes when she sees the expression on my face.

"*Samuella Wright.* Is there something you've neglected to tell me?"

* * *

On Friday, I'm sitting in my office staring at the clock on my computer. It's 9:58 a.m. We agreed on 10 a.m. just in case he got out a little late.

My calendar is empty for the first time all week, so I should feel relieved. Instead, my chest is in a vice.

I open my notebook and flip to the Baseline Collective tab. I always do my brainstorming on paper once I have solid information to go on. There's something about arrows, underlines, boxes, and circles that makes it all come together for me.

The phone buzzes once with a meaningless notification, and I nearly jump out of my skin. *Get a grip.* At exactly ten-oh-one, I flip the phone over and dial.

It rings twice.

"Hey," Justin says, a smile in his voice like he's been

waiting too. "I'm just pulling out of the gas station. Perfect timing."

"Perfect," I say, then laugh. "You already said that."

He chuckles. "How are you?"

My skin warms. "Good, and you?"

"Hm. Okay, we're avoiding the question."

I grin. "I'm tired. There, is that what you want to hear?" If I were telling the whole truth and nothing but the truth, I would say it was the most awake I've felt all week.

"That's better, yeah."

I *am* starting to feel some concern over this whole situation. The past four days gave me time to come to terms with the fact that I'm very interested in Justin in a not-so-professional way. I can't stop thinking about that kiss. Both of them, actually. And every time I think I may have rationalized each of our interactions into *see? He likes you, too!* I remember that moment at the restaurant, flirting with the waitress. Or him talking to women every time I see him at the pickleball club. *Which hasn't happened since before the tournament, even though I've been there three times this week.*

Justin is a major flirt, and I'm not convinced he wouldn't have done everything we did last weekend with any warm body who happened to be crashing on his sofa bed.

"Are you excited about this weekend?" I ask, rolling the trackpad on my mouse.

"I am."

"We're avoiding the question?"

He blows out a breath. "No, it's just . . . last weekend was so fun. I'm going to be flying solo this time."

Did he think it was fun because of our friends or because of me? "Is anyone from Smash Point going to be there?" I ask.

"No. There are a couple of guys I used to play with in California—"

"Wait, you lived in California?"

Justin tells me about his college days, how he ran track for UCSF. How his parents moved to Colorado during his sophomore year, and after he graduated with a business degree, he came out here to help them open up Smash Point.

I ask him about school, dating, his siblings, and then he insists I tell him about mine. There's not much to tell since it's only my brother and me, but I describe the designs we came up with for his wedding invitations and how I'm planning to fly out to Kauai for the wedding in June.

When I talk about college, I don't mention Adam. Not because I don't want Justin to know, but because I don't want to be a downer. It's hard to bring up death by suicide and not have the conversation take a turn.

I jump when someone knocks on my door, then straighten in my chair when Garrett walks in. "Oh, hey, Justin? Just a sec." I put him on mute. "Hey, what's up?"

Garrett leans against the door frame. "We're walking down to Olive and Finch for lunch. Alecia said you might want to join? She's hung up on a call and said you weren't answering your texts."

I search for the time on my computer screen. Eleven-forty-five? Holy shit. We've been talking for almost two hours and haven't once discussed a marketing plan.

"Umm, I think I'm going to have to pass. I'm on a call with Baseline Collective."

Garrett's eyes widen. "Solo account?" I nod, and he raps his knuckles on the wood. "So you're applying for the promo, then."

"I was thinking about it."

He smiles. "Good for you. That's great, actually. I think you'd be a good fit."

"Thanks." I give short answers, hoping he'll get the hint and leave. When he finally does, I fumble for my phone charging cord because apparently I'll be needing it.

thirteen

IT'S BEEN ONE DAY.

The longest day of my life.

Except for Monday through Thursday, which were also the absolute worst.

Based on my experience in the Springs, I'm positive Justin's been crazy busy, considering he doesn't have Calder and all of us to help this weekend. Still, by late morning, my restraint frays.

I open our text thread. Close it. Open it again.

Me:

Hey, I'm emailing you a few different color schemes. No rush

I don't need to announce it, but I'm secretly hoping he'll respond at some point so we can talk.

An hour passes.

Then another.

I finish cleaning my apartment, then head to Smash Point to meet Brooke and Rachel. Alecia and Calder have some day-date thing they're doing, and as I'm driving over to the club, I realize it's the first time in months that I didn't feel a twinge of jealousy at something like that.

After a couple of hours of open play, I'm back at my apartment, about to eat a Trader Joe's salad, when my phone rings.

I see Justin's name and immediately snap it up. "Hey."

"I figured calling was easier than typing."

My whole body settles at the sound of his voice. "Great idea." I remember making fun of my brother when he was constantly on the phone with his girlfriend—now his wife. Oh, how the mighty have fallen.

"How was day one?" I ask.

"Absolute chaos."

I ignore my salad, grab my water bottle, and settle into the couch. "Tell me about it."

Justin covers ball shortages, some altercation that nearly went to paddle blows, and a kid who threw up in front of the registration table.

I'm crying from laughing so hard by the time he finishes. "Where are you right now?"

He grunts like he just sat down. "In my room."

I want to ask if there's anyone else there, but think better of it.

Then he says, "The hotels here are cheap. I got a room to myself for half the cost of the last one."

A tight knot in my chest unwinds. "Well, it was a suite."

He sighs. "True. The sofa bed there was better than the bed I have here."

He would know. "Good food at least?"

"Ah, I'm about to treat myself to a gas station egg salad sandwich, so . . ."

"Wow, really treating yourself." I adjust the pillow behind my head. "But at least you didn't get anyone pregnant with your order."

He laughs out loud. "Man, I love you."

My breath catches in my throat. He was laughing when he said that. It sounded very much like a "Bro, I love you" kind of comment, but just the idea of him meaning it sends me into a tailspin.

I'm so screwed.

Justin clears his throat. "So, I looked at the colors you sent."

I exhale, thankful for the segue. "Yeah? What did you think?"

"Are you ready? I promised all the unfiltered thoughts in my head."

My anticipation cannot be overstated. "Go for it."

"Loved the mustard yellow and forest green combination. Really reminds me of those vintage hockey jerseys or the shirts with the lined sleeves. What are those called?"

"Varsity T-shirts?"

"Yep, those are the ones. Love the teal, though, too. It's my mom's favorite color. I like that it's a little muted, kind of reminds me of Hanging Lake. Have you hiked that?"

"No! I was going to visit last summer with some friends, but then we found out they switched to a reservation system. It was all booked up."

And we're off again. We talk about favorite vacations, best ski resorts and passes, and my stomach is growling by the time we wrap back around to the tournament with Justin saying, "I don't know if this whole Four Corners thing was a good idea."

"No?"

He draws a deep breath. "Colorado Springs was great, but this one . . . I don't know. Hard to turn much of a profit. Just didn't get a lot of interest."

My brain lights up, and everything I've been thinking about since Justin told me what he was working with comes pouring out. "I don't think you understand how amazing it is that you've gotten so much organic reach. You probably already know a lot of this because of your degree, but I wondered if you had standard operating procedures in place?"

"I have some, but that's the biggest reason I haven't hired more people. It's too overwhelming to figure out what to train on."

"Absolutely. But I think if we went through and categorized your tasks . . ." I walk him through a step-by-step plan of how we could get him organized. Then suggest that if he could offload most of those lower-level tasks, we could work on creating a content strategy and getting his socials more consistent, working on relationships with clubs and players, since that's his biggest strength.

"You shouldn't be doing admin work. Anybody can do that. You need to focus your time and energy where your strengths are," I finish.

There's silence on the line, and my stomach drops. "Sorry. That was—ignore me. I got excited and—"

"No," he jumps in. "I love all of that."

It's the second time he's used that word with me. I'm starting to like it. A lot.

"It's stupid, but hearing you talk like that . . . I think I've been lonely in this. I don't miss Prestige, but I do miss having a team. Someone to bounce ideas off of. To brainstorm with. This is really nice."

Warmth blooms beneath my ribs. It sounds idyllic to be able to work from home. To be completely flexible and set my own hours. But if someone like Justin, one of the most extroverted people I know, can feel lonely as an entrepreneur, I don't think my personality would have a chance of thriving.

"Where are you staying?" I ask.

"Tiny hotel near the courts."

We lapse into easy back-and-forth, and the conversation stretches another thirty minutes before we hang up.

I love all of it.

fourteen

ALECIA and I survive our first two days of the repositioning sprint. After a meeting with Garrett and Megan where we discuss the changes I could expect if I was offered the promotion—theoretically, of course, since I still had nothing to show for my solo account—Justin's texts on Wednesday feel like an oasis in the desert.

ME:

> Meet at the airport Friday?

JUSTIN:

> No, I'll pick you up

Me:

Oh and bring a dress

Like a nice dress?

If it has pockets, it doesn't count

I show Alecia the exchange over dinner at Linger on Wednesday night, and we brainstorm what kind of event would require me to dress up.

"Maybe he just wants you to wear a dress." Alecia takes a handful of our sweet Cajun appetizer popcorn.

"So he made up an event for it?"

"I mean, that would be hot."

I snort. "Or creepy."

"I doubt anything he does at this point will freak you out."

I laugh, but deep down, I know she's right. Anxiety's been building in me all week, and I haven't been able to pinpoint what's triggering it. Of course, I always start with Adam. This time of year is always hard, with less daylight and colder temps, then add in all these weird feelings with Justin, and I was bound to have a little bit of a meltdown.

But even after journaling, I can't seem to get to the root of it this time. It's like I'm playing with opposing sides of a magnet. Every time I get close, I slip past and end up right where I started.

"How did the meeting with Garrett go?" she asks.

"Great." I dive into the details, sharing how I'd be in

more of a managerial role. Approving designs rather than creating them myself. Managing our team and bringing in another team late summer. Paper and Pixel is set to double revenue again this year, and they want someone on board who's ready to scale.

Alecia listens and nods, but when she says, "That sounds amazing," it lacks her usual exuberance. I don't call her on it. It's been a long week for both of us.

We slog through the next two days, and Arizona comes fast. Justin picks me up right on time, and despite an awkward hug where we both turn our heads the wrong way, we manage great conversation all the way to the airport.

After getting through security, we stop for breakfast, then wait at our gate for boarding. It all feels easy. Like—well, like traveling with Alecia.

When I get annoyed with a TSA agent for making me put my bag back through because there was a single foil granola bar in the front pocket, Justin laughs and accuses me of being an attention hog. When he forgets his cell phone in the little bin, I grab it, don't tell him for ten minutes, then hand it over when he has a panic attack on the train.

Good times.

When I tell Alecia all of this in a text message at the gate, she responds with,

I'm being replaced!!!

And I'm just enough of a jerk to be a little self-satisfied, knowing that she understands how I've felt the last few months. But then I get over my cattiness and text,

> First of all, never. Second, thank you for teaching me what true friendship is

She sends a crying emoji. Which means she's actually crying because she refuses to send one of those otherwise.

My nerves are acting up when we get on the plane. I walk through the obvious. *I'm nervous about flying.* Always true. *I'm worried Justin won't like the mock-ups I have of the logo and branding kit.* True. Since he's not picky, I feel like I have to be uber-critical for the both of us.

Again, I slip past the knot at the base of my spine. What am I missing?

Justin drops into the seat next to me and hands me an earbud. "I have a surprise for you."

"Does it involve using this? Because I don't put other people's headphones in my ear."

His eyes sparkle, and he pulls a Q-tip from his pocket. Making sure I'm watching, he opens the little alcohol swab they handed him at the door, presses it into the cotton swab, then cleans out the earpiece.

"Does it pass inspection?" He hands it to me.

It's clean as a whistle. "That's the nicest thing anyone's done for me."

Justin barks a laugh, then pulls out his phone and holds it between us. "I downloaded six episodes of New Girl. Should take us from gate to gate."

"Don't jinx us! Knock on wood right now."

He looks around, then smirks and drops his gaze to his jeans.

I want to kiss him so bad, it aches. Instead, I roll my eyes, put the earbud in my ear, and tap play on his phone screen.

Such a damn flirt.

* * *

Justin prepared me for the room earlier in the week. It's just the two of us, and the hotel didn't have suites, so he got a King with a pullout since it was on some deal that made it fifty bucks cheaper than the rooms with two Queens. He's already told me there's no way in hell I'm sleeping on the pull-out, so I don't argue the point when we check in.

We spend the afternoon and early evening making marketing decisions. It takes half the time I expect because I'm used to clients hemming and hawing over options. Justin picks a logo within seconds. He opts for the array of colors with teal, and the tagline "Your Community Courts" is his instant favorite. He doesn't even need to see the others.

That night, we go to a Mexican restaurant in Scottsdale with some of his pickleball friends. The place explodes with color. String lights zigzagging across the ceiling, paper flags fluttering with the ventilation, and bathroom stalls wrapped in Valentine's paper with Cupids dangling over both sinks.

The tournament crowd packs the room. I didn't realize when we agreed to this, it wasn't just our group attending. Minnie sits two booths over with people from Prestige—I recognize them from the Springs. Notably, Finn Johnson isn't present.

Justin's hand finds mine under the table, and my whole body relaxes. It's the feeling I had when Alecia and I were trying to go without sugar for a month. We got one cheat day a week, and my day was Sunday.

Touching Justin feels like Sunday.

I don't know if it has the same effect on him, but he seems more than happy to put on a show. He leans in, laughs, then sweeps my hair behind my ear.

I should probably check to see if Minnie is watching, but it doesn't occur to me once.

fifteen

ON SATURDAY, I insist that Justin give me a job. Just like Albuquerque, he's running this thing solo besides the facility staff, but here in Arizona his registrations are full. He gives me one of his extra Baseline Collective hoodies, and I check people in, hand out wristbands, and help them find their courts.

I'm a little too smug when I see Minnie walking around in a huff because one of their Prestige banners ripped during transport. It's not like they don't have seven other ones to choose from.

Finn is on the courts that morning for another exhibition, but he doesn't parade around with Minnie like he did in Colorado. So that's interesting. Not that I want to spend my time obsessing over her or the drama, but it is a little like a train wreck. Hard to look away.

When I sit down to watch a few games, I notice a boy, probably around eight or nine, rotating between the first three courts. He's holding a paddle, and every time a game finishes, he finds his dad and goes up to the net to dink.

It's adorable.

His dad is playing in one of the lower divisions, and when he makes it to the finals, his son is glued to the court, holding on to the chain-link fence.

But he also keeps looking over at the Prestige courts. At one point, he perks up. I follow his line of attention to see Finn waltzing through the doors. The boy stares, forgetting to watch the game for a few points as he watches Finn walk down the aisle between courts and stop at the Prestige table.

"Quite the little fan." Justin stops next to me.

"I know. It's so cute."

Justin leaves my side and walks up to the boy, leaning down to talk to him. His mom walks over from one of the benches, and Justin introduces himself, then motions over at Prestige. The woman nods, and he motions for the kid to follow.

I frown, wondering why in the world he's voluntarily approaching Minnie. Finn's already gone, attracting a small crowd at the back of the venue, and I realize that Justin is talking with his ex to get an autograph. He's putting aside all of his pride and asking her for a favor when all she's done is criticize him and flaunt her success.

Something opens up inside me, crashing wide like a failed dam.

Minnie takes out her phone and makes the call. Finn walks toward the table a few seconds later, and when he arrives, he reaches out to shake the kid's hand. He signs the paddle, and when he hands it back, the smile on the boy's face is pure elation. Finn ruffles his hair and says something that makes everyone laugh.

Justin thanks them both, then turns and walks the boy back to his mom. He walks back to me, and I hug him. I'm about to say something about how there's no way he's the loser in this relationship, when he lifts his hand, and the scent of mint and hemp hits me.

My breathing quickens, my hands starting to sweat.

The hand cream.

Emotion rolls over me in a wave, and I murmur something about needing to find a bathroom. I spin and head down a hallway off the main court area, following a small sign with an arrow. The sounds of the tournament dull behind me. I pass a door marked STAFF ONLY. Then round the corner only to find a series of conference rooms. Have I really not used the bathroom here today? I don't see how it could be at the back of the venue, but what other options are there?

My hands are shaking as I turn to go back, but at the corner, I pause when I hear raised voices.

A woman's voice says, "I'm not asking. I'm telling you."

A man answers, exasperated. "You can't keep doing this, Minnie."

I nearly swallow my tongue and press myself flat against the wall. Ridiculous because if anyone walked down the hall, they'd see me easily. But it still feels a bit safer to take up less room.

I shouldn't listen to their private conversation, but where would I go? If I walk out now, they'll know I heard some of it. Is that a better option than waiting and sneaking out after they're done with whatever this is?

Minnie sniffs. "He doesn't get to walk away and make me look like—"

"This isn't about you looking bad!" The man cuts in. "It's not about Prestige or your numbers. This is about Justin."

Everything in me goes still.

"Of course it's about Justin. That's why we did this in the first place."

The man scoffs. "Yeah, well. I'm sick of playing your game. You told me you'd get good visibility on this tour, but half the sponsors have dropped out, and the spectator numbers—"

"I'm aware, Finn," Minnie snaps.

He pauses a moment, then says, "I'm not going to pitch a fit over this, but consider our contract ended."

"Finn—"

"Tell people I had to go home for a family emergency or something, I don't care what you say as long as it doesn't damage my brand."

"But we still have Salt Lake—"

"I'm not coming to Utah."

That shuts her up. At least for thirty seconds. "I can make an addendum. Pay you more—"

"I'm done, Minnie. I'm sorry. This whole make your ex jealous thing? Not what I signed up for. I was willing to do it when the numbers made sense, but at this point, I need to cut my losses."

I have to clap a hand over my mouth to hide my gasp.

Finn and Minnie? Not a real thing. And Prestige? Not as perfect as they purported to be on socials.

"I love him, Finn."

"I know."

"I just—" She sucks in a breath, and I can't tell if she's crying? "Ever since my brother died, I can't be normal. I get so scared, and then I—" She growls in frustration. "I act like a total bitch!"

Finn doesn't say anything.

Minnie's voice is high and tight when she continues. "I just want him back. For me, for Prestige. He brought in over half of our sponsors, and I've done everything I can think of to keep them, but they don't like me as much as they like him."

"They like you just fine."

"No, they don't! And I don't know what I'm doing! I'm failing at Prestige, I can't even pull off a successful fake relationship—"

Finn cuts her off, and their voices lower. After a few hurried lines, he murmurs something that sounds a lot like, "I'm sorry," and then the hall is silent.

Her words ring in my head. *Ever since I lost my brother.*

I wait until Minnie's heels click along the polished concrete. When the sound disappears, I cautiously peek around the corner.

Then I rush to find the actual bathroom. Because I think I'm going to throw up.

sixteen

JUSTIN:

Where'd you go? You okay?

I stare at the message until the screen dims. My thumb hovers, then I answer.

Helping out at the desk

I hope that buys me more time. I can't think, can't feel. Minnie's words pulled tight on that tangled knot in my chest, and it's choking me.

I'm a garbage person.

I purposefully tried to piss Minnie off, and I know she likely wasn't aware of the hate in my heart, but I know it was there. I wanted her to feel small—wanted her to eat the words she'd thrown at Justin.

It turns out, she's just like me.

I jump in and work. I do anything and everything that takes me away from the courts because I can't face Justin right now. By the time the day ends, my body feels hollow. I have at least ten texts from Justin when I walk the block back to the hotel and rush to the room.

I'm going to take a shower. I'm going to crawl into bed and—

Justin grabs the door when I push it open. "Where the hell have you been?" He pulls me into the room, presses both hands to my cheeks, and searches my eyes.

And I can't hold it back a second longer. My eyes well, my face pinches, and I start to cry.

"Hey, shh." Justin pulls me to his chest, and I sob into his shoulder. It's ugly and raw, and I can't make it stop.

"Sam. *Sam.*" He whispers my name, stroking my hair and rubbing my back. I cling to him for dear life.

We stand like that for what feels like an hour until my breathing finally starts to settle. "I'm so sorry," I say, not sure exactly who I'm apologizing to.

"For what?" He kisses the top of my head.

"For not texting you back. For taking off—"

"Stop, it's fine."

"It's not fine. None of this is fine." I pull back and swipe at my cheeks, but Justin won't let me fully escape.

"What isn't fine?"

"That I made Minnie feel like shit!" Fresh tears leak out of my eyes, and I soak them up with the sleeves of Justin's hoodie. "Did you know she lost her brother?"

Justin's eyes widen. "What?"

"Yeah. She lost her brother. And Prestige has lost half its sponsors. She and Finn aren't even a real thing—"

"Wait, slow down. *What?* How do you know all of this?"

My face twists with another wave of emotion. "Because I heard her talking with Finn in the hall."

Justin pulls me toward him again, walking me the few steps to the edge of the sofa bed. He sits, then tugs me forward so I can sit next to him. But as my body hits the mattress, a loud crack makes me gasp.

The bed collapses sideways, and Justin grabs onto me, rolling so I don't slam into the end table. We end up on top of each other. Half on the floor, half on the now broken bed frame.

I stare at him in shock. I want to laugh, but I don't think I'm capable of it.

The bed is broken. I started breaking down in the middle of a pickleball tournament, then cried like a crazy person, and now *the bed is broken.*

Emotions swirl in my chest like some toxic concoction, and I don't mean to do it. It doesn't make any sense. But Justin's face is inches away from mine, and he's warm and solid beneath me, and I just want to forget that the last three hours happened, and I remember how I thought of nothing the last time we were in this position.

So I say, "Will you give me your best kiss? Please?"

His breath comes in short bursts. "You want me to kiss you?"

I nod, a fresh wave of tears pressing against the backs of my eyes.

Just like the last time, he touches my cheek. I shiver, and his pupils flare. "I don't know if this is the best idea."

I tense, his words dousing every inch of heat under my skin. I push up, rolling to my hip.

"Sam—"

"No, you're right. I don't know what I was thinking."

"Sam, I didn't—"

"I'm going to take a shower."

I turn away as fast as humanly possible because I'm crying again, and I don't want him to see.

seventeen

THE BATHROOM FILLS WITH STEAM, and I can't strip off my clothes fast enough. I step under the hot water, pressing my forehead to the cool tile.

He's right. That would've been a terrible idea, and now he probably thinks I'm mad, which I'm not. I'm just—

I don't know what I am.

I'm sad.

Sad that I hurt another person. Sad that another person is hurting in the first place. Sad that I can't seem to communicate it in a way that isn't hurting Justin, and sad that . . . I have no excuse to be here in this room with him anymore.

We don't need to pretend. I don't need to be all over him at the tournament tomorrow, and I might not get to hold his hand again or kiss his cheek when we say hello, and maybe he won't call me anymore, and—

"Sam?" The door to the bathroom opens. The shower has a curtain, so I'm not worried he can see me.

I clear my throat. "Yeah?"

He doesn't answer.

"I'm good. I'll be out in a few."

"I just—"

"I promise. I'm good."

Another long silence. "I'm going to get DoorDash. Qdoba okay?"

I want to say something witty like it's better than gas station egg salad, but I don't have it in me. "That's great. Thanks."

By the time I get out and towel-dry my hair, I feel a little more human. I pull on my old clothes because I didn't think to grab new ones. When I step out into the room, Justin's sitting on the bed, takeout containers set up in front of him.

He motions for me to come sit, then passes one over.

I cross my legs under me and take off the lid. I don't feel like eating, but I know I need to. We watch an episode of *Frasier* and don't turn it off when it transitions to *Will and Grace*.

At some point, Justin cleans up our trash and closes the blinds. I say something about getting my own room, but he doesn't acknowledge it, just pulls down the sheets, lifts my legs, and tucks me in.

I come close to a laugh and tell him I still have to brush my teeth. He steps to the side, waits for me to use the bathroom and change into my shorts and tank top, then repeat tucks me in before stripping off his shirt and climbing into bed next to me.

We lie next to each other in the dark. His breathing slows, and I try to guess when he falls asleep. I think he's fully out when he shifts under the covers.

"Every thought in my head?" he murmurs.

The room closes in around me, and my lungs feel like slashed tires. "Mmhmm," I manage.

He draws a deep breath. Blood rushes in my ears, and even though I'm lying down, I feel lightheaded.

His voice is rough when he says, "I'm falling in love with you, Sam. I know I said it kind of as a joke the other day, and I'm not busting this out because you're sad. But I don't know if I would've had the balls to admit it if you weren't sad, so." He shifts again, and his voice gets a little closer. "You're hilarious and loyal and kind—"

I make a noise in my throat, and he reaches for me. "Stop. I get what you said earlier about Minnie, but you weren't doing that to be a jerk. You did it for me, and I don't think I've ever had someone stand up for me like that before. It sucks that Minnie's going through a hard time, and I'm going to find her tomorrow and say something. I don't know what, but something."

Justin breathes deep and reels me in, threading his legs with mine. "I didn't kiss you earlier because I still don't know if you want me, or if this is just a game to you."

"It's not a game." I press my nose into his neck. "But Justin—"

"It's okay, you don't have to say anything back. It's been what, three weeks? Shit." He drags his fingers through my hair. "I feel like I've known you my whole life."

I slide my hands up his chest, my whole body buzzing. Now that he's said all of that, it feels ridiculous that I've kept my own thoughts and feelings inside of my body. I've barely admitted anything to Alecia even though she can read me like a book.

My turn. "Every thought in my head?"

He sighs with relief, dropping his head next to mine. "Yes, please."

I swallow hard. If he can tell the truth, I can. "In college, I had a best friend named Adam . . ."

I fill in the gaps I left out during our car conversation last week. I tell him my fears, that when I love someone, I'm not good enough to see what's under the surface. That I worry about my friends, my family. That's probably why I jumped in when I saw him and Minnie in the hall because deep down, I'm still trying to save people.

"You use the same hand cream he did." I lean back and reach for his hand, bringing it to my cheek. The scent washes over me.

"I can stop."

"No." I shake my head and press a kiss to his palm. "It's good for me to be reminded." I close my eyes, and the tears that come now are nothing like the ones from earlier. They're slow and peaceful.

I don't think I'll ever fully be over Adam's death, but that doesn't mean I can't find peace. That I can't think of the good when something reminds me of him instead of wishing for something I can't have.

Because there are so many good things I still get to have.

"I think I've been falling for you since you ordered a burger at that restaurant in Colorado Springs."

Justin lets out a surprised laugh and pulls his hand from mine, wrapping it around my shoulders and dragging me back to his chest.

"Or maybe when I first saw you shirtless." I smile into his neck, the rumble in his chest vibrating through me.

"You thought I was a frat boy."

"Maybe I didn't know I have a thing for frat boys."

"Well, you aren't normal people." He slides his hand up the back of my tank top. "Hey." He pulls back, and even though I can barely see his silhouette, I know he's looking at me. "I'll always tell you what I'm thinking. You won't have to wonder if I'm struggling, okay?"

I believe him when he says it. For all his happy-go-lucky

energy, he told me when he was doubting himself. He told me when he needed help with marketing. More importantly, he didn't bristle when I made suggestions or wanted to jump in and help build his business.

"I don't think I want that promotion at work," I say.

"No?" He spreads his hand over my lower back.

I shake my head. "Going through this process with Baseline reminds me how much I love working with clients."

"Well, I'm probably an anomaly."

I laugh, squirming against him when he runs his fingers up my spine. "I'm talking about the *design* portion, not the clients themselves."

"But the clients do make a difference, right?" He tips my chin up and brushes his lips over mine.

I can't remember what else I was going to say.

He grins. "Sorry, I interrupted—"

I kiss him again, exploring the lines of his back, the slopes of muscle. "I want you," I whisper, and he cradles my head in his hand, breathing me in, kissing across my jaw and down the pulse in my throat.

"This is the 'and stuff' I hoped you meant," I say.

Justin surfaces, a smile in his voice. "What?"

"When you said we could talk about marketing. *And stuff*. I was hoping you meant this kind of stuff."

Justin gives a full belly laugh. "You caught that? I felt like such an idiot. I don't know why I gave such a weird pause—"

I pull him down and crush my mouth into his. My hands explore his chest, his arms, and when he moves the strap of my tank top to kiss my shoulder, I'm a goner.

I'm falling, falling, falling, and I love every terrifying second of it.

eighteen

MY BRAIN CLICKS on like a light switch at six o'clock. It takes me a moment to orient myself, but when last night floods into my head, the only thing I can do is smile.

Justin's arm is thrown over me, and when I roll to my back, his hand flexes over my stomach. "You're up," he murmurs, still half asleep.

"Sorry, didn't mean to wake you."

He grins, his eyes blinking open as he turns to look at me. "Please. Wake me." He grabs my hip and rolls me over until I'm lying on top of him. The room is still dim, the light a blue-gray coming through the small gap in the curtains.

I kiss the tip of his nose. "I really want to stay here with you."

Justin threads his hands in my messy hair. "But?"

"I think there's something I need to do."

His brow twinges. "Work?"

I shake my head. "At the courts." I pull my legs up to straddle him, pressing against his shoulders to sit on his hips.

"If you're wanting to get out of this bed, you should probably not do that." Justin's eyes drop, taking in my body under the thin strip of fabric that is my tank top.

I drop another kiss on his lips, then scramble off as he tries to clasp my thighs. He rolls to his side and watches me pull on my leggings. "If you're going down there, maybe I'll come and drill. Get in a workout."

"I'll show you a workout."

He laughs out loud. "She says as she leaves me alone in bed."

Justin gets up and throws on shorts and a T-shirt, grabs his pickleball bag, and we walk down together. It rained a little last night, and the air smells humid. Not at all what I'm used to in Arizona.

The venue doors are unlocked but the lobby's empty, lights still low. The courts stretch out ahead of us, rows of fences and nets.

"Want to play for a bit when you're finished with . . . whatever mysterious thing you're doing at seven in the morning?" he asks.

I pause, thinking that over. "Have we ever played together?"

He shakes his head. "You're too good for me."

"Ha!" I wave him toward the ball machines. I'm still figuring out how to navigate the team aspect of pickleball. I've never played with a set partner, and I'm definitely not good enough to partner with people like Justin and Calder. I've probably been too hesitant to set up games because most of my friends at Smash Point, courtesy of Alecia, are in those intermediate and advanced levels.

But I have been drilling with Rachel and Brooke. And how else will I get better, right?

I head for the staff room behind the registration desk

and call out, "I'll play when I get back. If you'll let me borrow a paddle."

"Wait, you're leaving?" Justin looks up as he wrestles with the outlet to unplug a ball machine. I assume he's already asked permission for that at some point.

I wink, then duck through the door. There's one staff member there, scrolling on his phone with a coffee the size of a small child.

I knock lightly. "Hey, quick question."

He startles and straightens. "Sure."

"One of the Prestige banners ripped yesterday. Do you know where it ended up?"

He winces. "Are you with Prestige?"

Based on that response, I'm guessing he got a chewing out yesterday. "No, just wanted to help."

"Oh, okay." He doesn't try to hide his surprise. "Well, yeah, I can show you. I think it's still in the trash pile in the warehouse." He walks me past the bathrooms to what looks like a supply closet. When we walk through the door, a vast space with shelving and storage opens up. It smells like cardboard, which I'm sure they see a lot of here. Boxes of paddles, clothes, and balls.

He walks me over to a pile of cut plastic wrapping, pallet ties, and one rolled-up banner sitting on the top of the pile. Black vinyl with their logo, the bottom corner torn clean through near the grommet.

I crouch, pulling it free, and run my fingers over the damage. Okay. Not catastrophic. The vinyl itself is intact. The rip is localized, probably from tension at the corner when someone over-tightened the zip tie. The grommet's torn out, leaving a crescent-shaped tear that looks worse than it is. No ink damage. No creasing.

Fixable.

I carry it back into the light and spread it out on the floor, smoothing it flat. When I was a kid, my dad's real estate office sponsored my brother's school. They needed new library books or something. In return, he got to put a banner up on the schoolyard fence, and after a weekend of brutal Colorado wind, half of it tore off. He didn't want to spend another four hundred dollars to print a new one, so the three of us fixed it on a Saturday.

Never thought that knowledge would come in handy.

In my head, I'm already inventorying what I need. Clear vinyl repair tape would be ideal, but heavy-duty duct tape would work in a pinch if I reinforce it properly. Replacement grommets would be better, but that's a longer shot this early in the morning.

I glance at my watch. The twenty-four hour Walmart is twenty minutes away based on my search in the bathroom this morning.

I explain my plan to the staff member, then jog back to the courts. I wave Justin down, and he pauses the machine, sweat already darkening his shirt.

"I'm going to make a quick run to the store. Need anything?"

He walks over to the fence and wipes his face with the towel hanging from the side of his bag. He's hot like this. All working hard and panting.

Justin looks up at me and grins. "Condoms."

My smile splits my face. "How many?" I tease.

"Probably the fifty pack. We *are* staying one more night," he deadpans. I laugh and am already walking away when he calls out, "Magnums!"

I snort. "Glad you clarified! I was about to search up a Big and Tall store!"

I ignore the weird look I get from the staff member at

the front and focus on Justin's goofy grin that makes all of my internal organs liquify. *Why does he have to run a tournament today?*

I'm regretting my choice to leave the bed this morning as I walk to the front, but I have to go through with this now. I hope Minnie appreciates my sacrifice.

I catch an Uber to the store, and it's surprisingly quiet. I thought after hours was when Walmart got real crazy. I grab a cart and head straight back to the home improvement section.

One roll of clear Gorilla Tape. Heavy-duty zip ties. A small grommet kit with a hand punch—total jackpot. Scissors, just in case the ones at the club suck. A microfiber cloth.

Total damage is under twenty bucks—well, before the fifty pack of condoms—and I'm back at the venue before the parking lot's even full.

I set up shop on one of the empty courts, banner laid flat with my supplies lined up. Time for a little banner surgery.

I wipe down the vinyl around the tear so the tape will adhere properly. Then I cut a strip of clear tape longer than the rip, rounding the corners so it won't peel, and lay it over the damaged area. I press from the center outward, smoothing air bubbles with my thumb. Flip it over. Repeat on the back side, sandwiching the vinyl. The tear disappears, reinforced but invisible from more than a foot away.

Next is the grommet.

I measure the placement so the hole won't stress the repair and punch cleanly through both layers, then insert the grommet halves. It feels good to wield a hammer even if I can't hit as hard as I want to.

When the metal's bent, I test it by tugging.

Solid.

I thread a zip tie through the new grommet, cinch it to the post just enough to hold without tension, then repeat on the top corners to distribute the load. When I lift the banner, it hangs evenly, logo smooth, damage completely unnoticeable unless you know where to look.

Gotta say, having only done this twice, I'm pretty damn good at it.

It takes me a minute to prop the door open, but I finagle the banner out and carry it to the Prestige desk. It's not heavy, just awkward.

The staff member who helped me earlier walks over and whistles. "Looks brand new."

"Well, just don't look too close."

Justin's face is unreadable as he pushes through the gate on his court and walks toward us. He looks up at the banner, then back to my face. "You did this?"

I nod, not sure what to do with my hands. "Minnie was upset yesterday. It got ripped—"

"No, I know. I heard her griping about it all morning." He takes a step closer. "If I wasn't so sweaty, I'd make out with you so hard right now."

I laugh. "It's not a big deal—"

His hand shoots out and he pulls me, laughing, against his damp shirt. "Nope. Too bad. Doing it anyway."

nineteen

THE REST of Arizona goes by in a blur, and that fancy dress I brought? Yeah. We don't end up using it.

We change our flights and stay all day Sunday instead of leaving that morning. It gives us a lazy morning, brunch, and six blissful hours in our hotel room together before we have to head to the airport.

And then when Justin drives me home, he makes a quick trip to his place to grab his things, and comes over to stay for the week.

After all, we have so much marketing to discuss before Salt Lake City. Which we barely get done because it's really hard for me to want to leave my bedroom and go to work.

I had no idea that Baseline is Justin's sole source of income. He's doing well enough that it's profitable after only a year and a half. He runs local leagues, which I had no idea about, creates programming for other clubs, and then runs tournaments and events across the country. Last fall, he ran tournaments in Idaho, Washington, and California.

This isn't just a little hobby like Minnie asserted. This

business has legs, and I'm more excited about work than I've been in years at the prospect of helping his small company grow.

By the time Friday hits, I've rush printed banners, table-cloths, pens, pickleballs, paddle weights and wraps, and clip-on sweat towels.

I work for a few hours that morning and pick up the last of our things, then take a dolly to the elevator where Calder and Alecia are waiting to help me load my car up. Rachel, Brooke, and our other Smash Point friends are meeting us at the airport.

I toss Alecia a pickleball, and her eyes widen. "Stop. You didn't—" She squeals when she reads the writing on the side, then hands it to Calder.

We wait on the edges of our seat for him to read the word "Frederick" emblazoned on the side in black ink.

It finally computes, and he laughs. "When did you get this printed?"

Alecia points at me, and I shrug. "I needed a sample before ordering."

"You two." He points between us like we're about to get spankings.

Alecia runs over and squeezes me tight. "You're the best, Sam."

I sigh dramatically. "I know."

* * *

Salt Lake got all the snow we were hoping for over the last week, and it's an absolute bear hauling all our supplies into the pickleball club Friday night.

Eight checked bags. Eight.

There are pros and cons to going all out on the branding.

The moment we get the gear inside, our group shifts into work mode. Brooke and Rachel start tearing open packaging. Calder checks in with the front desk and finds out where we can stash extra swag. Alecia walks a slow lap, scanning for the perfect location for our desk and banners. Not that there's much to choose from since Prestige will be taking the other half of the facility as usual. I'm actually surprised Minnie and her team aren't here yet.

Justin kneels down and helps me sort banners, table-cloth, signage, swag, tape, and zip ties. I brought the tape, grommet kit, and scissors from Arizona just in case.

Brooke holds up a bag of paddle weights. "These are honestly hot."

Justin's smile splits his face. "You all can have whatever you want. Just take it."

"Within reason!" I shout when Brooke takes off with the bag.

Justin smirks at me, then plants a kiss on my cheek before reaching for a banner stand.

After only another forty-five minutes, we're putting the final touches on the swag table, and Alecia says, "So, I hear you pulled your application for the promo."

I wet my lips. "Yeah. I just—"

"I think it was absolutely the right call."

I blink, spreading out the paddle weights. "You do?"

She nods. "I didn't realize it was going to be so managerial. You're so good on the client side—"

"Right? That's what I was thinking."

"Plus with all of this Baseline stuff—"

"Ugh, I'm loving it. I want to learn more about systems so I can help Justin set up some really tight work flows."

Rachel and Brooke come over to drop off a few more balls they found in one of the bags. Alecia sets a handful of pens in a cup and grins at me.

"What?"

She turns to look at Justin and Calder straightening the last banner halfway down the courts. "I think we all need to acknowledge that I totally set this up."

Brooke and Rachel laugh.

My jaw drops. "You said—"

"I know what I said, but c'mon. You guys are perfect together, and I—"

"That was not your intention!"

"I don't know, I think it might've been."

"Hey, we need some credit, too," Rachel says. "That night we walked in on you two making out—"

"What?!" Alecia's practically salivating.

"Oh yeah," Brooke jumps in. "And how they sat stiff as boards, pretending they were watching a show."

They bust up laughing, and my cheeks heat. "We weren't making out. He was just . . . showing me how he kisses."

That leads to an uproar, and I can't help but join them.

Alecia sighs. "Well, I'm just saying, if I wouldn't have forced you to sign up for pickleball night—"

I snort. "You're insufferable!"

She boops my nose. "A simple thank you would suffice."

I try to slap her butt, but she dances out of the way. "You're welcome!" she sings, motioning for Rachel and Brooke to join her at the front to help Calder clear the last of our trash.

Justin hears the commotion and looks over, his face lighting up when our eyes lock.

Hm. Don't mind that at all.

I will tell Alecia thank-you.

When she isn't so cocky about it.

I step away from the table and pull out my phone to take pictures. We don't have someone assigned to social media yet, so our entire group is on duty this weekend. Clips, interviews, podiums, we're going to capture all of it. I may have stalked a few pages, including Prestige, with Justin over the last week to get an idea of what we want it to look like.

I snap a picture of the swag table, then turn to get a clip of Justin and Calder when someone approaches.

I drop my phone when I find Minnie standing in front of me. She's dressed like she always is for an event. Clean and put together. Her eyes scan the space, landing on our branding first. The banners. The backdrop. The table behind me.

She doesn't say anything, but her mouth tightens at the corners. Then she folds her arms over her chest and looks at me. "I know you fixed my banner."

It's not an accusation, but there's no warmth in the statement either.

I nod once. "I was happy to help."

Minnie's eyes narrow. Her gaze slides toward Justin, then she looks back at me and sniffs. "Thanks."

"You're welcome."

Her mouth twitches like she's going to say something else, but then she turns and walks back to her team hauling in boxes for Prestige.

I don't know what I was expecting. A heart-to-heart? Some acknowledgment that she's been trying to get back in with my boyfriend?

Then again, I'm not admitting that the first time we met, Justin and I barely knew each other's names.

Probably best that we leave it at this.

Justin appears at my side a second later. "You okay?"

I nod. "Yeah."

He puts a hand on my lower back, and I turn to him. "I'm glad I repaired what I could."

Justin grins. "Wait, me? Or the banner."

I laugh and brush a kiss over his lips.

We gather the group and take a picture before heading back to the hotel. Alecia and Calder suggest a restaurant close by, but Justin turns them down.

"Nope. We have plans."

I frown. I was not aware of any plans this evening.

When we enter the lobby, Justin jumps in front of me and drops into a crouch.

"What—?"

"Just get on!" he laughs.

Maybe it's all the relaxed energy after seeing our vision come to fruition, but for once, I don't question it and do as I'm told.

Justin hoists me up like I weigh nothing to hoots and hollers from our friends. I yelp, arms locking around his shoulders.

His laughter rumbles through his chest.

"What are you doing?" I ask, breathless.

Justin doesn't answer, just hauls me over to the elevators. We go up two floors, then stride down the hall to the room we checked into a few hours ago.

But instead of opening the door, he sets me on the floor. "Wait just a second." He swipes his key card, barely opening the door and slipping inside. "Wait," the door opens an inch. "Do you have your key?"

"Yes, I have my key."

He grins, then closes it. "Come in when I tell you!"

I laugh, completely clueless. I'm imagining possibilities for what could be behind that door, and then I hear the TV turn on. What the hell?

"Okay! Come in!" Justin yells.

My heart races as I scan my key and push the door open.

Justin's there, leaning against the kitchenette with his shirt off. I start to laugh, then see the box of microwave popcorn on the counter along with two pairs of fuzzy socks in Baseline colors and a couple of my favorite San Pelegrino's.

My throat thickens.

"Is that—?" I give him a look and walk into the living room. The sofa bed is pulled out and made, and *Friends* is playing on the TV.

"It's the one where Ross says Rachel's name at the wedding." Justin steps up next to me.

"I love this one."

He kisses my temple. "To be fair, I got lucky on that one. I was worried I'd have to turn on Law and Order or something."

I laugh and turn into him. "This is the most romantic thing—"

He kisses me, long and slow, then pulls back. "I'm still pissed at Rachel and Brooke for coming home early that night."

I sigh against his lips. "I wanted to punch them in the face."

He grins and pulls me closer. I melt against him, breathing in that soft scent he wears mixed with that hint of peppermint.

I'd like to think I could've eventually figured this one out on my own, but let's be honest. Sometimes I need a little help from my friends. Both the ones right here next to me and the ones I still miss.

Justin rests his chin on my head and lets out a satisfied huff. "Welcome home, Sam."

129

epilogue

IN MAY, the doors to Smash Point are propped open and fresh air flows through the building as we play. We're on Court Six, which has become our default because it's close enough to the "peanut gallery" benches where people can heckle, but far enough from the juniors' area that I'm not accidentally taking out a small child with my mishits.

Justin spins his paddle in his hand. "Okay, if I get pulled wide like that, you need to shift over and cover the middle."

I sigh. "Yeah. I know."

"Hey." He grins, wrapping his fingers in my ponytail. "It's just a game."

"But I'm making you lose."

He scoffs and kisses my forehead. "I never lose when I'm with you."

"Stop making out and play already!" Alecia snarks from the other side of the court.

"They're killing our momentum," Calder mutters.

We finish the game—score isn't important—and walk off the court to get water. Drew jogs up to the sideline with his paddle bag bouncing against his hip. "Hey, Justin. You want to partner for the tourney this weekend?"

"Back off. I already claimed him," Calder says, and Drew laughs.

"Boys, boys, you're both pretty," Rachel says, stretching since she and Brooke get the court next.

"Next time?" Drew says and Justin nods.

"For sure. I'm in."

Just as Rachel and Brooke are about to walk on the court, Spencer, one of the Smash Point employees, runs up.

"Hey, Rach, there's a new kid up there who wants to join juniors. Can you come talk to his dad? They just moved here, I think."

Rachel's face lights up. "Absolutely." She nods to us. "Be right back."

We watch her jog up to the front, but it's Brooke who says "Daaaammmmn" when we all realize who she's talking to.

A man puts out a hand to shake. He's dressed in firefighting gear. No jacket, but the turnout pants, boots, and he has a radio clipped to his suspenders.

Beside him is a kid, maybe eight. Small. Hands shoved into his hoodie pockets.

"Okay. Now I wish I was running juniors," Brooke says, and Alecia snorts.

"You still could."

Calder shakes his head. "Too obvious at this point."

Brooke smacks his shoulder.

"He's a unit," Justin says, and I nod in agreement.

We're still watching as Rachel returns to the group a few minutes later. "What?" She looks between our faces.

Brooke smirks. "How was that conversation?"

Rachel gives her a look. "Seriously?" She picks up her paddle. "He's just a dad looking for a program for his kid."

"What about something for him?" Brooke says. "He's probably tired after a long day—"

Alecia snorts, but Rachel ignores her completely.

"Get your ass on the court, partner," she says. "I'm ready to play."

Calder and Alecia take their places since winners stay, which means Justin and I get to watch this one.

"You're getting so good," he says. "Those blocks were crazy."

"Well, I have good teachers."

Justin rubs his stubble over my cheek. "Stay at my place tonight?"

I grin.

"Since we have a lot of marketing to discuss."

I cackle, and he snatches me before I can pull away.

"C'mon, Sam. Focus. Our friends are playing."

Such a damn flirt.

Cindy Gunderson is a voice actress and award-winning author. Since she has commitment issues, she writes both sci-fi and fantasy, as well as contemporary romance and women's fiction under the pen name, Cynthia Gunderson.

When she is not typing away in a quiet corner of her local library, you can find her traveling with her family, narrating audiobooks, or happily digging in her garden. She loves acting and performing, beating her kids in card games, and playing ultimate frisbee with her handsome husband, Scott.

Cindy grew up in Alberta, Canada, but has lived most of her adult life between California and Colorado. She currently resides in the Denver metro area. Cindy holds a B.S. in Psychology from Brigham Young University.

Cindy's first novel Tier 1 was awarded First Place in Science Fiction at the 2021 CIPPA EVVY Awards and her women's fiction novel Yes, And was honored with the Indie Author Award's first place prize for the state of Colorado, 2023.

also by cynthia gunderson

Standalone Novels

Yes, And

I Can't Remember

Let's Try This Again

Holly Bough Cottage

The New Year's Party

Sugar Creek Series

One Last Christmas, Love in Audio

Canadian Played Series

Against the Boards, Called for Icing, Stickhandle with Care, On the Power Play, Guarding Home Ice, Offside Attraction, Drop the Mitts, The Dying Seconds

Campus Confessions Series

The Breakaway, The Save, The Comeback

Smash Point Social Series

The Big Dink, The Setup

Find signed books and discounted bundles at

www.CindyGunderson.com

Instagram: @CindyGWrites

Facebook: @CindyGWrites

TikTok: @CynthiaGWrites